RING

Michelle Lerner

T0244131

bancroft
press

RING

Cover Design: Christine Van Bree

978-1-61088-627-7 (HC)
978-1-61088-628-4 (PB)
978-1-61088-629-1 (Ebook)
978-1-61088-630-7 (PDF)
978-1-61088-631-4 (Audiobook)

Published by Bancroft Press
"Books that Enlighten"
(818) 275-3061
4527 Glenwood Avenue
La Crescenta, CA 91214
www.bancroftpress.com

Printed in the United States of America

ADVISORY

This novel discusses suicide. If you or someone you know is in crisis and needs immediate help, contact the National Suicide Prevention Lifeline. Call or text 988, or chat at 988lifeline.org.

If you are deaf or heard of hearing, you can contact the National Suicide Prevention Lifeline via TTY at 800-799-4889.

Things might seem impossible right now, but talking about it can help. Call or text 988. It's a confidential helpline, and it's available 24/7.

For Shire, who started me on this path;

for Laura, who encouraged me;

and for Brian, who accompanied me.

PROLOGUE

SNOW

Taking that first step out of the hut sounded more difficult than what would come after. Of course, this was just speculation. It's not like I could ask someone at the final pillar as they took their penultimate breath.

Which seemed harder to me? Leaving my apartment, or whatever might happen in those last seconds that lighten the body by seven-tenths of an ounce? Did it matter?

I had a friend once who was almost 98. He had a tumor in his lung. He wanted to talk to me about what his last moments might be like. I told him I was sure he had time left.

Now I wondered why I couldn't talk to him, when the last moments he was asking me to imagine were his, not mine. I guess I thought no one was ever ready. Not at 98. Not with cancer.

Not even the suicides.

BEFORE SANCTUARY

Union Station

Union Station in Winnipeg was huge. Entering through the glass doors at the bottom of the concrete facade, I had the sense of walking through a portal. The space inside was open, round, and clean, with a high circular skylight that looked like a miniature firmament sitting on the globe of the waiting room.

I don't know what I'd been expecting, but I suppose something quiet and discreet. Something out of the way. Winnipeg was not that place.

I had a few hours before the train left for Churchill. There were no empty benches, and I was so exhausted I considered lying down on the floor. Instead, I sat on a bench occupied only by an elderly woman, in the hope that, once she left, I could lie down or at least rest there against my backpack.

On the plane ride here, I'd felt no fear, at least not of flying. I had always been so scared of it, until the trip last summer to claim Rachel's body. On that flight, I had barely noticed being in the air. But I hadn't been sure if that was just due to the shock, or what to expect on the flight yesterday from Madison to Winnipeg. So I'd carried my bottle of Xanax in my pocket, planning to take as much as I needed before the final leg of my trip to Attawapiskat, at which point I would throw away the rest—the Seven Pillars Society doesn't allow tranquilizers.

This trip was the first time I'd left the apartment since the funeral. In truth, I'd hardly been out of bed in months. I couldn't even find the energy to stand in the shower, had resorted to getting into a bathtub when required by exasperated friends who stopped by to try to get food into my mouth and stench off my body. What I remembered most about the months after Rachel's death was the olive and white of the apartment walls, and the rough woven texture of the mustard-colored curtains in the bedroom. The feel of the comforter between my fingers as I pulled it over my skin, often as a shield against Susan's constant repetition of all the minutiae we knew about Rachel's last day. I'd begun taking the Xanax all the time; it was no longer just for flying.

But yesterday, on the flight to Winnipeg, I'd found I didn't need it. Fear of flying has to do with fear of death. After Rachel died, I guess this fear just disappeared. When the plane landed, I tossed the pills.

It didn't take long for me to realize that was a mistake. After the flight, as I lay in the hotel bed, unable to sleep, I remembered that you're not supposed to suddenly stop taking medication like that, that it has to be tapered. That it can even be dangerous to stop cold turkey.

There was nothing I could do about it at that point.

I was already used to being awake on and off during the night. I hadn't had a normal circadian rhythm since Rachel's death. I was rarely awake or asleep more than three or four hours in a row. Though I'd lived through many days since my daughter died, I couldn't admit they were of the same nature as when she was alive—similar length, similar weather. That I was moving through the doors of the same successive hours as the people I saw walking by the window of my apartment. The days seemed to pass through me rather than the other way around.

I slept, drug-induced, at odd times. The hours stood still on top of me, little demons with weights pinning me to the bed. The stillness wasn't natural, but it was complete. Somehow my chest had continued to move, and air entered my lungs—my only source of amazement for months.

But in the hotel room last night, without the Xanax, the feeling was different. It was a clearer-headed, pulse-racing awakeness that was not just an interlude between sleep, but something actively opposed to sleep. I lay there at least half the night with my heart pounding in my chest.

The snow outside the window had calmed me. It was dark, but I could see it coming down, feathery and light against the glass. There was a bright blur in the sky that could only have been the moon behind clouds.

The benefit of not falling asleep had been avoiding the moments after waking, when I'd usually forget, and then remember.

RACHEL

Rachel was a clear brook, transparent, deep. Every pebble dropped straight to her core.

She was the purest metal, conducting every spark that touched her, taking everything in and passing on the charge.

Once when she was nine, she told her teacher she couldn't concentrate because of singing outside the window. She was sent to the nurse, then the counselor, then home with a note that she needed a psychiatric evaluation. But, she insisted, someone really was singing, loudly. She took me there the next day, to the tired grass below the window of her classroom. Bending down, she held out her arms with her hands on the ground while a cicada climbed up her shirt, trilling.

There was before Rachel, and there was after Rachel. There were twenty-three years in between. The twenty-three years that were Rachel.

When they found her car in the desert, Susan was convinced Border Patrol was responsible for her death. Rachel was working with a grassroots group driving food and water to migrants, and was proud of her work. Then we stopped hearing from her. Then they found her car. Then they found her. The investigation by local law enforcement found no evidence of anyone else's involvement and ruled it an accident or suicide, with heat exhaustion the cause of death. That Rachel either had been affected by the heat while trying to get to a particular spot to meet someone, or that she had just walked out into the desert alone as a way to kill herself.

Susan didn't believe any of it, was sure the investigation was tainted because of Border Control's likely involvement, that Rachel wouldn't have done this to herself, that she had left no note, that she was experienced in the desert and the desert heat and couldn't possibly have been so careless as to strand herself and succumb to heat exhaustion.

It's not that I thought Susan was wrong. I just wasn't sure she was right and I had no energy to fight, no sense of what could possibly be done since the essential event could not be changed or set right. Susan flailed and raged, took my resignation about the investigation's conclusions and my shriveling withdrawal as an offense, contacted lawyers and human rights organizations. There was always a new suggestion of where to look, who to contact, what to ask, but none of it ever led to any answers.

She pursued every detail, wanted to talk through it every minute of every day, over and over, shuffling papers on her lap, rereading out loud each detail of the same reports, asking me the same questions. While she talked, I lay in bed with the demons on top of me, facing the wall. None of it came to anything. Six months after her death, there was no more information than in the first days after she was found.

It's hard to explain, but by that time it almost didn't matter what had actually happened; I was devastated to the marrow of my bones. There was nothing left. She was gone. She had walked through some door, willingly or unwillingly. The need to understand why eventually ran itself aground in the stunned silence inside my head. There were no longer meaningful points of view, things to comprehend or argue about. There were just ideas like piles of sand that people moved from here to there, separated out into smaller piles, stood in front of, gave names to, fought about. I would say I stepped around them, except I hardly got out of bed.

Because, really, the piles were made of quicksand. Miniscule, nondescript, meaningless spots of quicksand. All around my bed. Susan and the other people entering the apartment dragged them in. My bed was solid, so I stayed there and looked at the ceiling while they talked in the other rooms. I don't remember if I got up when Susan moved her last box out the door. To be honest, I don't really remember her leaving.

Sometimes I try to think of Susan before and during Rachel. Because it doesn't seem fair to only think about the way she acted after. But every time I try, all I see is the drawn skin on her face, the plowed furrows on her forehead, the lines at the sides of her eyes and mouth. For every rung I climbed down inside myself after Rachel died, Susan climbed up and out, anger emanating from her the way heat rises off the pavement in August.

There must have been a moment when we crossed each other's latitude. Maybe it was the day they found Rachel's body, since I remember Susan's fingers gripping the flesh of my sides. I know she wailed, but in my memory, she was silent, her mouth large and moving without sound, her fingers gripping me tight.

After that we lived in two different climates. I've been told everyone grieves differently. Which presupposes that each person is still there, intact in their personhood and personality, engaging in the action of grieving as an experience or a process. But I think grief takes its own form as it consumes a person from the inside, devouring whatever preexisted.

How it looks from the outside depends on how fast it does the devouring, how completely, and with what kind of energy. By the end, Susan and I were just vessels for grief, its fingers reaching out through our previously human bodies. In Susan's body, the grief was hot and could not stop running. In me, it was a glacier, and the ice filling me became me. Cold to the bone, there was too little of me remaining to stand in her way as she left.

The Train

The train from Winnipeg to Churchill would take two days. It was a crazy way to get to Attawapiskat. It took me farther north than I needed to go and added more than a day to my travel. But Rachel had been insistent that we go to Churchill as part of the trip north we'd been planning, because she wanted to see polar bears, and to satisfy her desire to see every kind of wilderness.

It was close enough to where I was going that I wanted to see it on this last journey I was taking, maybe as another way to remember her, to be with her. I didn't have the energy to go looking for polar bears, but I could sit on a train and look out the window for both of us. As strange as it sounds, a part of me felt like she was calling me there, like the decision to take this roundabout route was her idea.

This train in particular had excited her imagination. Traveling more than five hundred miles through boreal forests and the subarctic region of northern Manitoba, it boasted a car with floor-to-ceiling windows and panoramic views, a dining area, and sleeper cabins. The only land route to some of Canada's northern-most communities, it promised sightings of wildlife like black bear, caribou, and wolves. And it passed through towns hundreds of miles apart from each other, some with human population numbers like ninety-eight or forty-three. Rachel wanted to know what it looked like, what it felt like, to be that far north with so few humans and so much space. She'd experienced it in the desert, and she wanted to experience it in the tundra.

Taking the trip now, alone, I didn't feel the need to buy a sleeper cabin. It didn't matter to me if I slept, or when, or in what position. I chose a reclining seat by a window, put my backpack on the rack above, and sat. If Rachel had been with me, if we'd taken this ride together as we'd planned, I would have settled in with a book and a cup of tea and alternated between reading, looking out at the view, and talking to her about the landscape and our mutual feelings of anticipation. But since Rachel's death, I hadn't been able to read a thing but the guidebook, and I wasn't anticipating anything but the feeling of snow beneath my body. Before the train pulled out of the station, I pulled the guidebook out of my backpack and put it on my lap.

GUIDED

In the weeks after Susan left, I mostly stopped eating. Her friends took turns coming by to check on me, to try to get me out of bed. Jenna was the only one I really talked to, and even with her I said very little. One day while she was in the apartment, she found the guidebook that Rachel and I had been using to plan our trip, though we'd never gotten around to picking a departure date. Jenna brought the guidebook to the bedroom and handed it to me without comment.

I don't know if she was just trying to interest me in something—anything — or if she actually remembered that Rachel and I had intended to travel there. If she did remember, I'm not sure why she assumed it would help me to think about this trip we'd never take, why it didn't occur to her that it might just make me worse.

But after she left, I sat up in bed, a pillow behind my back against the headboard, blankets over my legs. The book, tattered and dog-eared, was 102 pages long, with a white laminated cover that was cracked the way a windshield cracks—a small thick line with tiny spiderweb-like emanations in every direction. The title, *An Outsider's Guide to James Bay*, was printed in large light blue letters in a sans-serif font. Below it was a faded photo of dark blue water and white snow.

Most of the book was basic travel information for getting to and around the area. Flights into Fort Albany, visits to Akimski Bird Sanctuary, canoeing Moose River. Reading it somehow made me feel closer to Rachel, and it opened some window on the suffocating stillness of my mind. I flipped through the book aimlessly, unable to concentrate on more than a few sentences at a time, until I saw the breakout box in the last chapter. That's where I settled that night, and for all the time since.

The Seven Pillars Sanctuary, the guidebook said, was founded by the Seven Pillars Society, which was incorporated as its own religion. The Society had built a small colony at an undisclosed location near, but not in, Attawapiskat. The book said the Swampy Cree First Nation government in Attawapiskat had nothing to do with Seven Pillars.

The guidebook chapter contained a map of the lower western shore of the bay, but the sanctuary was not on the map. Nor was there any contact information for the Society or the sanctuary. Oddly, in this guidebook filled with tourism information, the Seven Pillars breakout box was written almost as a story rather than as a guide to a real place.

I don't remember what went through my head the first time I read it, because I've since read it so many times, and talked to Samu and Catherine, so it's hard to sort out which conclusions I came to when. This is what's clear:

the idea of a place in the snow with no roads or nearby towns, where one could stay in silence and receive training for weeks or months before heading out into the snow, where each pillar in the snow represented a journey through a layer of the self, where the seventh pillar was the end of the line, and where all that was left was you, the snow, and the air—this was the only place where it seemed tolerable to exist, even if the expected span of existence there was limited. All time is limited, after all, and how long it seems to last is dictated by many things, the ticking of a clock being perhaps the most objective, but least relevant, measure.

For the first time since Rachel died, I wanted something. I wanted to go there. I wanted to walk out into the snow. I wanted to never come back.

In my condition, the task of finding contact information for the sanctuary seemed herculean. I wanted nothing to do with my computer. But eventually I got up, sat at my desk, and turned it on. I tried several direct searches with no success, but finally found a vague reference and, when I clicked on the link, was taken to a message board of a type I hadn't seen in a decade. The individual posts were cryptic and contained terms that the few users seemed to understand, but which meant nothing to me. Yet in the process of skimming the posts, I found a name, Catherine, and a phone number that appeared to be for the sanctuary.

I wouldn't talk to Susan, my own wife, but I called this stranger and left her a voicemail saying I was interested in becoming a devotee and walking the Seven Pillars. It took almost a week to hear back from her, during which I wondered if the place was real. The sanctuary's voicemail had no outgoing message other than confirmation of the number and the word "Namaste."

But she did call back. Catherine apologized for the delay and explained that the sanctuary had only satellite phone service, and all non-emergency voicemail messages got returned once a week.

When I repeated my interest in walking the seven pillars, she was friendly but emphasized that the central devotion of the sanctuary was not the Seven Pillar walk but the training that came before it, and I'd need to commit to that in order to be allowed to visit. As long as I completed the training, she added, whether I walked or not was immaterial to the sanctuary and its staff, which on further inquiry appeared to be only her and another person named Samu.

I must have sounded distressed, because she assured me that she and Samu would provide all the support needed to walk if that was what I wanted to do at the end of my stay. But she reiterated that the society only supports walking to the Seventh Pillar once a guest's mind is calm and settled, when the intention can be pure and certain. Walking without this would not be a religious rite, but simply suicide, and they could not support that.

After all, Catherine asked, if the only thing I wanted was to die, surely I could find a way to do that without leaving home?

NORTHERN LIGHTS

I knew the train would be slow, but it seemed to be crawling at the speed of someone walking, or maybe jogging. The guidebook referred to it as the slowest train in the world, which I had thought was hyperbole. But the track condition was terrible because of all the freezing and thawing. And with the temperatures increasing this far north at twice the rate as in the rest of the world, the problem had only worsened, even though at this time of year there was no thawing, only freezing.

We passed through forests of scrubby pines, riding on tracks that seemed invisible due to the snow-cover. As we made our way closer and closer to the tundra, the landscape opened up into flat expanses that were extraordinarily still. If I looked out to the horizon, it sometimes seemed that we weren't moving at all. This made my heart palpitate, so I focused my eyes on the near distance, which provided some sense of movement. I didn't need the train to move fast, but I needed to know I was getting closer.

The stillness inside me was remarkable for its comprehensiveness and consistency. Even without the Xanax, it was unmarred by bouts of crying or extreme emotion. All feeling had been carved out of me and disposed of, other than an interminable, squeezing ache in my chest that called my attention to every inhale and exhale. How that pain could exist in such silence was inexplicable.

Xanax had been the only thing that helped; it didn't make the ache go away or populate my thoughts or drop a pebble into the silence, but it clouded my mind enough to withstand it all for short periods and made me sleepy enough that I never had to remain conscious for long. Without the Xanax, I was awake and present to the physical pain of breathing. But I knew it was time-limited, that I was going to relieve it, that I might even join Rachel in some way, and that made it marginally bearable.

Then, on the second night, the lights came. I was the only one awake in the car. They took up half the sky and were different than anything I'd ever seen. Glowing green fingers curled toward the train, and at first my breath caught in my throat. But then, watching them, I felt the first peace, true peace, since Rachel. Because it was her, I knew, beckoning me. And because I was on my way

CHURCHILL

It looked like the whole town was there to greet the train, and maybe it was. The woman stepping off the train in front of me said there were fewer than a thousand permanent residents and not much to do, so the weekly train arrival was a big event. I wasn't sure who she was talking to.

When I entered the station, there were posters of polar bears everywhere, with contact information for adventure guides. There was also a kiosk advertising kayaking with beluga whales, but it was unattended. Kayaking didn't seem like an option in January at -29 degrees Celsius (about -20 Fahrenheit), even if anyone had an interest.

I exited the front of the station and the frigid air startled me. Winnipeg had felt cold, but this was something else entirely, and it took my breath away. Some parts of Wisconsin got this cold, but Madison almost never did, and it was hard to get used to. I saw a waiting taxi, a brown unmarked station wagon with a laminated sign taped to the backseat window, and got in.

The heat in the car blasted loudly. "Where to?" the driver tapped his palm against the steering wheel as I fumbled with my backpack, looking for my wallet.

"Can you take me to the closest hotel?"

"The closest one? It's not a great place. We have some really nice lodges— at one of them, you can sit in a heated glass dome on the roof and watch the aurora. You should let me take you there."

I considered it briefly, remembering the lights from the train and thinking about what Rachel would do, but I couldn't muster the interest or the energy. I knew that even if I went to that hotel, I wouldn't leave the room.

"The closest one is fine."

We pulled out of the train station and drove the few short blocks into town. The road was wide and dusted with snow, and lined with large, oddly squat wood buildings spaced far apart. A broad blue structure had a sign that said "Northern" and appeared to be a supermarket. An oversized dark green building sported writing across its façade announcing it to be a diner, seafood restaurant, grill, bar, and lounge. In the space between every business, I could see far out into the distance over flat, snow-covered land.

A gigantic gray sky hovered above the landscape, and occasional boulders or tufts of plant matter stuck up through the snow. A few people walked down the side of the road in animated conversation, didn't look at us as we passed.

We turned and drove by a series of small connected row houses painted in bright primary colors, an identical set of plain wooden steps leading up to each front door. After the jarring size of the businesses, the houses looked tiny and understated.

The driver stopped in front of a green building low to the ground, peppered with tiny windows. It looked like a miniature version of the multi-purpose restaurant we'd passed, but the sign indicated it was a hotel.

MIGRATION

The lobby, if it could be called that, was a small room stuffed with padded furniture, taxidermied animals, and paintings of wolves and arctic scenes. I had to avert my eyes to avoid the dead animals staring at me across the crammed space.

When I checked in, I took one of the dozens of brochures on the counter about seeing polar bears. I'd be in Churchill the rest of today and much of the next, and while I had no energy, it seemed like a shame to come all the way here and not see the bears for Rachel. When I lay down on the bed and opened the brochure, though, I could see that I'd arrived just after the bears' annual migration.

Churchill, being farther north and on the shore of the larger Hudson Bay, was not in the James Bay guidebook, and it hadn't occurred to me that the bears' proximity would be dependent on the season or to do any research about it. I'd done the bare minimum to get here and, it seemed, polar bears migrate in the opposite direction of what Americans would normally expect. When the bay starts to freeze in late fall, they congregate around town waiting for the ice to get thick enough to cross on their way north to hunt seals for the rest of the winter.

While they're known to wander right through town, necessitating a complicated alert system and a "polar bear jail" to hold them pending transport, people usually go out on monster-sized, guide-driven "tundra trucks" to look for them. With climate change, it was taking longer and longer for the bay to freeze, and so polar bear viewing season was extending into December, but not this late into the winter.

In spring, the bears would be back to den and have their babies near here, though because of changes to their hunting patterns, they were returning skinnier and skinnier each year, and fewer cubs were being born. The brochure encouraged tourists to try to see the bears before they entirely disappeared. At any rate, they were elsewhere now.

There was no food at the hotel. I didn't think about this until I was in the room lying on the bed, deciding that I'd read enough about polar bears. I felt hunger so infrequently that I required visual reminders. So many times in the past months, I'd gone at least this long without food, and I could do so again. But Catherine had said I needed to commit to eating regularly in order to stay at the sanctuary. I remembered I had a protein bar in my backpack.

Catherine had instructed me to buy the large internal frame backpack, bright red so as to be easily located in the snow. Also several specified layers of clothing and two pairs of specified boots. The welcome packet she'd sent me provided links for ordering them online. I had bought my supplies, and my ticket to Winnipeg, all without leaving the apartment.

When the backpack arrived, it was the brightest thing I'd seen since my metamorphosis into ice. It came in a box so flat I was unsure what it was. Jenna, visiting the apartment to try to get me to eat, brought it up from the vestibule, put it on my bed, and opened it in front of me with a car key, slashing through the tape and cardboard and pulling on the flaps. Then she stared blankly, and blinked a few times, at the cranberry fabric covered in thin plastic. I sat up and dragged the backpack from the box and out of the packaging, grabbed its flesh from both sides, and tugged outwards until it took the shape of an empty half dome.

I hadn't told Jenna, or anyone, about the Seven Pillars. She was visiting every week or so on a schedule worked out with a few other friends of Susan's. I'd known them for years, but I'd met them through Susan and they'd remained closer to her. She'd asked them for help; I was sure of it. My own friends had dwindled in recent years to colleagues I didn't socialize with outside of work. I wasn't talking much, and I wasn't leaving the apartment, but an enormous red backpack was now sitting on my bed. I sympathized with Jenna's confusion but told her only that I'd ordered it online and didn't want to discuss it. Then, unable to help it, I pulled the backpack to my chest and held it like a child.

For the weeks that followed, I slept with it in my arms, between me and the covers. It wasn't soft. I tried to imagine it was rough like skin, desiccated skin that's been out in the sun. But it was rough like synthetic cloth woven for outdoor use. I don't know why, but it comforted me, and I couldn't let it go.

When I'd thought about leaving, I was worried someone would follow me and try to stop me. I'm not sure why; it seems silly now. Jenna and the others were all frustrated. They wanted more than anything for me to leave the apartment.

So when I left, I taped a note on the outside of the door explaining I was traveling to see a friend who had moved to Canada and invited me to stay a few months, that I would have my cell phone but it likely wouldn't get reception, and that I was grateful for everyone ministering to me for so long and sorry I'd made it so difficult.

The day I left for Winnipeg, I remember thinking that I needed to eat in order to make it to the airport. But the kitchen had become foreign to me and, even faced with the upcoming expenditure of energy, I could not manage to put anything in my mouth to fuel my body. I found a bowl full of protein bars sitting on the counter, and I put them all in a side pocket of the backpack. I then hoisted it onto my back and almost buckled under the scant weight of a pair of boots, some clothes, a parka, and the bars. Because I was hardly eating, they had lasted until now, my overnight stay at this hotel in Churchill.

I pulled out the last bar and made myself eat it. While I chewed, I lay down on the hard double bed covered with thin duvets, and looked out the undraped windows at the snow.

I thought about how strange it was to be here without Rachel. Rachel was the adventurer, the one who never took a straight path to anywhere. She was gifted and had learning disabilities, and did everything her own way. She went to Prescott College, a small experimental school in Arizona with no grades and a lot of experiential outdoor learning.

God, she loved it. She learned to rock climb, spent weeks out in the wilderness with other students, navigating with a compass. It was almost impossible to live with Susan whenever Rachel was out backpacking like that; she'd get insanely anxious. I thought it was good for Rachel, and was happy she was doing it. It's not that I never felt anxious when I knew we wouldn't hear from her for weeks. I just thought she had the right to do the things that interested her. Sometimes I even wished I could do them with her.

While Rachel was at Prescott, she started volunteering on weekends with a group that brought water and food to migrants crossing the desert near the U.S.-Mexico border. The organization was run by a doctor who kept getting arrested by Border Control, then prosecuted for aiding undocumented migrants, just for giving them water and food to survive their journeys. Susan worried Rachel would get arrested too, but she never did. Then, once she graduated, she moved on to a more radical group that also tracked Border Control's movements and tried to help migrants avoid encounters with them.

At that point, even I occasionally got nervous and would ask her if she needed to be doing the hands-on pieces of this work, if she couldn't instead get involved in policy advocacy. But I always knew the answer, knew what Rachel's talents were and were not, what her restlessness was like, her dislike of rules. So I supported her in her ongoing arguments with Susan, viewed her activities as important to her developing in her own way, in the same way that when she was a kid, I'd always found her quirks fascinating and worth encouraging— her uncanny musical ability combined with her utter lack of interest in learning to play an instrument "right," the way she collected odd friends who came into her life like strays from various contexts and traumas, the way she failed to be impressed by authority of any kind.

All of it was completely opposite of my own personality and everything I'd done in my own life, but it all seemed so Rachel. I followed her the way a fan does, keeping up with what she did and where she went and who her friends were, out of fascination and interest and an utter amazement that the tiny infant I'd rocked in a sling had somehow developed into this incorrigible, strange creature.

Susan's reaction was very different, even when Rachel was little. Everything Rachel did either irritated or scared her. She loved Rachel as much, if not more, than any mother loves their child, but felt endlessly panicked by and involved in her choices. She wanted her to take advanced placement classes in high school, wanted her to pick a more traditional college, thought she should have a major.

When Rachel first started doing work at the border, Susan agreed that the immigration system was a carnival of horrors and that refugees and migrants crossing the border needed support, but she didn't see why Rachel needed to be involved so directly, and was terrified she was going to get hurt or killed. I tried to watch over Rachel in my own way, largely by goading her into planning trips that would involve me, to all the places she wanted to go, from Cuba to James Bay.

We went a couple of times, just her and me—Iceland one August, backpacking in the Grand Canyon during one of her October breaks from school. But mostly we talked about trips we'd take in the future and planned our routes in great detail. In the process, she would tell me things about her life that she didn't tell Susan. I never directly asked her to stop doing what she was doing. I think it was this, as much as my inability to keep searching for answers after her death, that made Susan blame me. Because, in the end she was right: Rachel really had put herself in danger, and I hadn't done anything to try to stop her.

Plane Wreck

After finishing the protein bar, I remembered that I had no Xanax, and that I might be stuck awake for hours. There was a TV remote control on the small bedside table, next to a brochure on things to do in Churchill. I didn't feel like reading any more, but watching TV sounded even worse. I picked up the brochure, reasoning that if I couldn't go out and see the town, I could at least look at pictures of it.

The front of the brochure highlighted the Itsanitaq Museum, which it also called the Eskimo Museum. This surprised me. From my guidebook, I'd gathered that the term was considered derogatory. I wondered who had written the brochure and decided to keep using the offensive term. Photos of tools, kayaks, and art were interspersed with pictures of a large number of stuffed dead animals. It seemed this area was big on taxidermy.

Inside, one pane focused on the history and demographics of the town, describing it as more than half Indigenous, mostly Swampy Cree, Chiepewayan, and Métis with a small Inuit community. While Indigenous people have inhabited and hunted on the land for more than a thousand years, the town was named after John Churchill, First Duke of Marlborough, who ran the Hudson Bay Company that set up the first permanent settlement right in the polar bears' migration path.

The next section of the pamphlet was dedicated to the Miss Piggy plane wreck, which, as far as I could tell, was an actual crashed cargo plane that had been decorated with graffiti and was now considered a tourist attraction. It was called Miss Piggy because it was overloaded when it went down. A satisfied visitor was quoted as saying she'd never before been able to walk right up to a real crashed plane. At this, I re-folded the brochure and put it back on the bedside table.

I hadn't watched TV at all since Rachel died, and wasn't sure I wanted to now either. But I was afraid of lying there clearheaded and awake so, feeling a rising anxiety in my chest, I turned it on.

It came into focus in the middle of a hockey game. I changed the channel to a CTV News program, in which a reporter was interviewing a resident of Attawapiskat about some kind of water crisis. The resident, a woman in her forties, sounded exasperated. "How can it be that in Canada today, there are so many Indigenous people who don't have access to clean water? First we couldn't drink it and now we can't even bathe in it? This is ridiculous."

The reporter nodded with a solemn look, then turned to the camera and explained that this situation in Attawapiskat once again exposed the failure of successive governments to end drinking water advisories in more than one hundred First Nation communities. She explained that instead of fixing the problem in Attawapiskat by building long-term water infrastructure, the federal government had decided to pump water out of a local lake and treat it with large amounts of chorine, which had combined with other elements in the water to create high levels of toxic byproducts.

The reporter kept nodding her head as she spoke, which I found distracting. She reminded viewers that Attawapiskat was the same First Nation that had chronic overcrowding from a housing crisis, the same community where, in 2016, eleven teens had tried to take their own lives on a single day, and more than one hundred in a matter of months. At this last statement, I sat up, but the reporter had moved on. "Federal spending on First Nations communities remains less than half of what is spent on non-Indigenous communities on a per capita basis, despite the cost of living being higher in northern communities than elsewhere in Canada, and despite the impact that underfunding has on the health and lifespan of citizens in places like Attawapiskat." She signed off and passed back to the anchor.

I turned the TV off. I didn't want to keep listening to voices. I didn't want to do anything. But, unable to clear the mental image of the hundred teenagers, I sat up and pulled the guidebook out of my backpack, got under the covers, and turned to the pages on Attawapiskat.

The guidebook said Attawapiskat is the home of 2,000 Cree. On one page, there were these statistics: 52% high school drop-out rate; 70% unemployment rate; no permanent doctors at the hospital; pregnant women required to fly to Moose Bay to give birth. On the facing page appeared a photograph of a smiling, stunningly beautiful woman about Rachel's age, looking right at the camera.

I turned the page. There were no permanent roads leading out of town. In the winter, a frozen path along the bay makes it accessible to a few other coastal towns. In addition, ice roads are constructed, leading out of town toward nearby diamond mines and mining settlements. I tried to imagine living in a place where the roads just end, instead of leading to other places. Rachel had driven her Toyota from Madison all the way to Arizona. What would it feel like to walk to the very end of a road and just stand there, looking out at a landscape unmarred by buildings or pavement? To know that one more step and you're outside of town, without another town for a hundred miles, or many hundreds of miles depending on the direction you faced?

If I'd said this to Rachel, even while resting in the hotel, she would have stood up and insisted we go find out. Because Churchill, too, had an end of the road. I had no desire to stand up, much less go for a walk. But even without Rachel to goad me, I would soon find out what it felt like.

Because this was where I was headed.

PLANE RIDE

The only way to get to Attawapiskat from Churchill was by propeller plane. Samu would pick me up at the airport and then and take me to the sanctuary, first via the winter road, which was made of ice, and then over a snowmobile trail that would take about two hours to traverse. With climate change, the winter road's season was becoming shorter and shorter every year. I'd had to time my trip carefully to arrive before any chance of thaw. Otherwise, the trip would be longer and more difficult and the possibility of snow melt could complicate my plan to walk. This had meant leaving for the sanctuary just a few weeks after I spoke to Catherine the first time.

The airport in Churchill, a small blue and gray building made of corrugated metal, had two runways and both were covered in snow. The taxi drove me right to the building, and I went in and walked up to the empty counter and waited for someone to come help me. An attendant entered from a door behind the counter, and I bought a seat on the noon flight to Attawapiskat. I paid for the ticket with cash. I still shared a credit card with Susan, so at some point she would know I'd bought a plane ticket to Winnipeg, but I didn't want my entire trip to be traceable. I'd taken out enough cash to pay for the train, the propeller plane, and my needs beyond that point, and had already sent the sanctuary a check.

The man behind the counter directed me to a metal folding chair in the single room where I would wait until boarding. I sat down about five seats away from two large white men in coveralls with the word De Beers stitched across the front. They were smoking, openly, inside the closed room. I looked around for "No Smoking" signs and, seeing none, glanced back over my shoulder to the attendant behind the counter, but he seemed unaware or unconcerned. The men's accents sounded American Southern, which surprised me. I couldn't place them more specifically, but I knew they weren't from up here. Even from five seats away, I could faintly smell alcohol emanating off them.

Every once in a while, one or the other would guffaw or snort. The one with brown hair and a graying beard turned his head and saw me watching. As he leaned into the other man's space, I thought I could hear the word "faggot" as the other man shook his head and said "dyke." I was surprised by the sudden surge of heat in my face, the clenching of my stomach. I stood up and moved to the outer perimeter of the room as the announcement came to board.

Walking out behind the building, I handed my backpack to the pilot as directed and climbed the stairs to the plane's doorway.

There were eight seats but only four other passengers. Besides the men from the waiting room, there were two Indigenous passengers, a young woman with a serious face and long dark hair tucked behind her ears, and a thin older man. They looked at me without smiling and sat down as far as possible from the coveralled men.

I had never been on a propeller plane and was surprised by the amount of noise. I sat by a window and could see the flat white ground passing beneath me, and when I looked across the aisle, I could see the ice and dark water of Hudson Bay which, the guidebook had noted, combines with James Bay to make the world's largest inland polar sea.

As we started to descend, I noticed a flat silvery band snaking through the white landscape, which I assumed was the Attawapiskat River. Out the window on my side of the plane, I could see a grid of streets with small houses and other buildings.

The Attawapiskat airport was really just a flat expanse of snow with a brown, almost windowless one-story building that looked more like a large storage shed. The pilot got out of the plane, opened the luggage storage compartment, and carried two suitcases and my backpack over to a window in the building. She then pushed them through a movable flap so that they disappeared inside. I disembarked onto the snow-covered runway and stood there, the cold air biting the exposed skin on my face.

I collected my backpack and walked to the road, where I waited. The air was still except for the fog of my breath. I continued to be surprised by the working of my lungs—that they kept inhaling and exhaling without any effort from me, even in the frigid cold. That it would, in fact, take some effort to stop them.

SAMU

Time passed. I didn't look at my phone because I didn't have anywhere else to be. The only concern was the quickly approaching darkness.

Then suddenly a motorcycle with a side car was coming toward me on the road. It slowed and stopped, and a man in what looked like fake leather chaps fastened over red snow pants got off, removed his bright red helmet, and smiled at me. "Lee, yes? I am Samu."

Samu had curly light brown hair the color and texture of muddy straw. His accent was unmistakably Hungarian. He sounded just like my neighbor whose daughter used to babysit Rachel. I don't know why, but I had expected Samu to be Cree. As this thought passed through my head, I realized I knew nothing about Cree names, and briefly wondered how I'd arrived at my assumption.

I didn't tell Samu any of this, but expressed surprise about the motorcycle, saying I had understood we'd be riding a snowmobile. He explained that the ice road along the river, called the winter road by the locals, is hard on the sled of the snowmobile, so when it's open, he leaves the snowmobile at the turnoff and rides the motorcycle into town. We'd ride the bike on the ice road for about 40 kilometers, which would take well over an hour because of the conditions. Then we'd get on the snowmobile for the final stretch to the sanctuary.

I had never ridden a motorcycle or in a side car. I watched Samu tie my backpack on and motion for me to climb into the sidecar, which I did.

Once out of town, we turned onto the ice road, which Samu shouted was literally made out of ice. He said they rebuilt it every December, mostly for the local mining operations, but it gave residents a few months of mobility beyond snowmobiles and planes and shortened the ride to the sanctuary. Lately, the construction had been more difficult because of the rising temperatures, and in areas where the road went over water or wetlands, the ice had to be artificially thickened by surface flooding and spray-ice techniques.

As a result, the ride was rougher. He told me not to be afraid of the large fissures in the ice, that the bike would go slowly and make it over the cracks just fine, but it would be bumpy. Since the side car was open to the air, Samu had given me an extra scarf to tie around my face, showing me how to leave just enough room for my eyes, and a visor to cover them.

Surprisingly, even with the scarf pulled tight against my mouth and nose, my lungs were still at it.

ICE

The road was, in fact, made of ice—thick ice, carved or flattened into an actual road, wide enough for three or four vehicles but with no lines or other markers. The edges were bordered by snow banks. I still couldn't understand how it was made, but the cold wind dispelled the question quickly. It was bumpy and Samu was right, there were very large cracks that sometimes looked like they ran several feet deep.

After an hour or more, I could see some structures approaching on the left. Samu slowed the bike and then stopped. He got off and asked me to exit the side car. A few yards off the side of the road was a wood shed with a padlock. Samu brought the cycle in. I could hear him doing something with chains, and after a few minutes, he emerged with a large snowmobile attached to a sled. He put my backpack in the sled, climbed onto the machine, and asked me to get on behind him and hold his chest. It wasn't far to the sanctuary, he said, but it would take some time to get there. He pulled his visor back over his eyes and I climbed on behind him and held on as he directed.

Though it couldn't have been later than 2:30 or 3:00, the light was already fading. Samu turned on the snowmobile's headlights and pulled out into the oncoming dusk.

SANCTUARY

Eventually the light faded to black on all sides except straight ahead, in the path of the headlights, and above our heads, where the stars were clear as lit matches. How Samu knew where he was going was a mystery. All that lay ahead, as far as I could tell, was snow. And now snow was falling as well.

At some point, after so many breaths into the vibrating night air, a hulking shape appeared in front of the lights, first small and nondescript, and then expanding in size until it became a wide rectangular one-story building with strange protrusions off the left side. Samu slowed the snowmobile and pulled up to a lighted door.

Standing in front of it was a woman with short black curly hair, light brown skin, and a slight padding of weight on her cheeks and torso. She wore a luminescent purple shirt under a heavy gray cardigan and, on opening the door, asked me to come in quickly so as not to let the heat out.

In the center of the room was the biggest wood stove I had ever seen. Made of black cast iron with a glass door displaying crackling red and orange flames, it was connected to a metal pipe going up to the roof. Catherine saw me staring at the stove. "We don't always use it," she said. "You'll see tomorrow. We have a large solar installation and geothermal heating, and we do a lot of the heating that way. The stove is supplemental, but it feels so good at this time of year, and it's so comforting to look at after dark. I'm always drawn to the warmest spot in the room. I like to say it's because my family's originally from Syria and not used to all this cold. But I was born in

Winnipeg, so really I think I just like wood stoves." She smiled.

The windows were small and unevenly placed, and because it was dark out, I couldn't tell how much light they'd let in during daylight hours, which were, in any case, somewhat scarce at this latitude and time of year. The wood floor was covered in places by bright woven crimson and cobalt rugs with geometric patterns, and in each corner were groupings of padded couches and chairs arranged in semi-circles. At the far end of the room was a doorless passageway leading somewhere else.

Catherine offered to take my parka and motioned for me to have a seat on one of the cushioned couches in the corner on the left. I sat down, feeling the cushion depress under my legs, which were still buzzing with the vibrations from the snowmobile.

She returned with a mug of steaming liquid. "Motherwort and sage tea," she offered. "It'll warm and calm you. It'll also help you sleep."

"Thanks. I don't even remember the last time I had something to drink."

Catherine looked displeased. "In this weather, you could have gotten hypothermia from dehydration. I know you probably don't care right now, but that's not the way to go. Trust me. While you're here, you need to stay hydrated, and you need to eat. I can tell you haven't been eating."

I felt the protruding bones of my face.

"But I don't mean to lecture you. And don't worry: We'll help you with all of this. For now, just rest, and in an hour, we'll have dinner. We eat early here. Samu will take your backpack to your room, and tonight you don't need to help cook. Just please sit and watch the fire. Tomorrow, we'll go over everything and you can start."

Before I could say I just wanted to go to bed, she was gone. As I contemplated lying down on the couch, someone came out of the passageway. Or, rather, more than one someone.

An angular, balding white man, who looked like he was in his sixties, entered with a dog following close behind him. The man had a thin rim of gray hair, and his skin looked lightly tanned, almost yellowish. The dog kind of resembled a border collie, slender with longish black and white fur and the outline of a white circle set off against the black on one side; short ears that flopped over; and a penetrating gaze directed right at me. It stayed within inches of the man's legs. I felt a new pain in my chest looking at the dog, though I didn't know why.

The man walked up to me. "You must be Lee. Catherine told me you'd get here this afternoon. I'm Robert. And this is Ring."

ROBERT AND RING

Robert sat down on a chair facing me. Ring jumped on the couch next to me and lay down, pushing the side of his body against my leg. I must have looked surprised because Robert said, "Please excuse him. He doesn't leave my side. Unless someone else's side is available."

I looked down at Ring, who seemed to have settled in for nap. I put my hand on his head and slowly dragged my fingers down his neck and back, parting the fur in little rivulets. He sighed.

Robert said he needed to help cook dinner, in the kitchen, which was just off this room, and if it was okay, he'd leave Ring with me. "Once he realizes there's food in the picture, he might follow me. But Catherine doesn't let me give him scraps in there so he's mostly lost interest in the production side of dining."

I didn't say anything, and Robert stood up to leave. "Before you ask," he said, "pancreatic cancer." He stood looking at me expectantly.

"I'm sorry," I said.

A look of slight disappointment drifted across his face. "Don't be sorry," he offered. "This place has helped me a lot. I've done a lot of healing."

"You're healing?" I asked, surprised. "The cancer's going away?"

"No, that's not what I meant." His brows furrowed as he shook his head. "The cancer won't go away. I'm walking the pillars in a couple of weeks, while I'm still able."

I looked at him again, and he turned to leave, saying "I'm sorry. You just arrived. You don't need to know the state of my organs. It's normally everyone's first question so I get it out of the way. I'll see you at dinner."

And with that, Robert left the room.

Ring's head jerked up and he watched Robert disappear through the passageway. At first, he seemed a little anxious, almost like he was holding his breath, and I thought he might jump up and follow Robert. But instead he turned and looked at me expectantly, like I'd been in the middle of a sentence and he wanted me to finish it. I put my hand back on his head and told him, "I'm Lee. What's a nice dog like you doing in a place like this?" Satisfied, Ring sighed again, dropped his head back down to the couch, closed his eyes, and fell asleep.

SANCTUARY

FOOD

The sanctuary's food was grown in three different greenhouses attached to the main building. Two hydroponic and one soil, kept at different temperatures through complicated systems involving solar panels, geothermal heating, grow lights, pipes, and gravel. Catherine explained it to me over dinner the first night: red chard, black-eyed peas, and salted raw tomato slices. They grew much of their food, didn't eat or use anything from animals. Food was central to the belief system on which the sanctuary was founded. The earth, an element of god energy, should provide everything we ingest, and in return we should work the earth with our hands, breathing in and ingesting the air and soil. The hydroponic systems were used because accessing sufficient soil was difficult and the hydroponics had large and consistent yields, but the food grown in actual soil had special relevance for nutrition and spirit, and so something from the soil greenhouse was included in every meal. In this meal, it was the chard.

Feeding oneself was a central tenet at the sanctuary, Catherine said. Thus, the first part of my training would involve working in the soil greenhouse and learning how to convert what I harvested into meals. I would start the next day. I felt some level of confusion. I understood that I was expected to eat while at the sanctuary, but I was surprised that, in a place where people were preparing to walk out into the snow, it would be important to learn skills around food production and preparation. I said as much, perhaps too bluntly. Catherine and Samu looked at each other, and then Catherine assured me that I'd understand more once I received some training, and that it would help me appreciate the food more. But I didn't want the food. I wanted only to lie down.

There were five people at the table, and Ring below it. Catherine, Samu, and Robert were on one side. On the other, I sat next to Viviana, muscular and Black with mahogany skin, dense clipped hair graying at the edges, and a weathered, almost military look. Maybe butch, or maybe non-binary, I wasn't sure.

Other than Catherine, the rest were silent as they ate. I picked up a single black-eyed pea on a tine of my fork and put it in my mouth. It had been so long since I'd had a cooked meal, I was surprised by the strong flavor and the warmth. I put the fork down, and then heard Viviana's voice for the first time.

"If it's hard for you to eat, you can drink your food. I did that for the first few days. You just blend greens and water with flax seeds and a little fruit, then keep it on you and take small sips all day. It helps."

I nodded. No one asked me anything at all. I briefly wondered what Catherine had told them, then realized, as with most things, that I really didn't care. In more ways than one, we were in all in the same place.

Night

If you associate darkness with night, it's difficult to name what occurs here from mid-afternoon to mid-morning at this time of year. It doesn't make sense to say that the period of darkness starting before four p.m. is night, especially the hours when we work and train. Or eight in the morning when everyone has been up for hours. Darkness is more like the base of existence here, bracketed by periods of sunlight that mark the actual passage of time the way nights do in other places.

When I woke up, I had no idea how long I'd been sleeping. It was, of course, still dark. In the apartment, it wouldn't have mattered what time it was, but I got out my unconnected cell phone and turned it on. It was four a.m. Technically, then, still night. But I knew I wouldn't be able to fall back asleep, and Samu had said I could go to the kitchen as early as five and he'd be there ready to help me start my first day.

The walls of my room, like those of the main room, were made of wood boards, though the ceiling was lower and made of sheet rock. There were three things in the room. Four if you counted the drapes on the small window. The single bed was in the middle, under the window, and on the right side was a rocking chair on top of a circular green rug. No dresser, or mirror, or TV. There were hooks on the back of the door for clothes, as though no one would have more than a few pieces. And, of course, I didn't.

The bed was firm, and the room was small and sparse. But it was welcoming. And it had enabled what was, for me, a surprisingly long interlude of sleep.

It had been so long since I wanted to get out of bed. I had expected that to be the difficult part of being here, the expectation that every day, without fail, I would report to the kitchen in the morning. But somehow I felt the urge to stand up, put on my sweater, and go find Samu. Maybe it was the lack of Xanax. Maybe it was wanting to get it over with so I could get closer to walking out in the snow. Regardless, at four a.m., I was on my feet.

I opened the door to a dark hallway but could see a light at the end, past the main room, at the door of the kitchen, and I made my way there. I was wearing socks but no shoes, as I had left the pair of boots I'd been wearing in the main room by the wood stove and had not had the energy to get the other pair out of my backpack, string the shoelaces, and put them on.

The boards under my feet felt solid and differentiated, and I noticed a slightly different sensation when I stepped on cracks between the boards. It was the first time I remembered thinking of my feet since Rachel. I hadn't been using them much, and they hadn't seemed very involved in what I was going through. But, like my lungs, they appeared to still be with me, living their own life and making what they could of the new surroundings.

When I entered the kitchen, Samu turned around and nodded at me but didn't smile. I was suddenly nervous that maybe I should have waited until closer to five, that perhaps I was not welcome at this time of day. But he was just measuring some kind of ground seed into a bowl and I could see him counting to himself. When he finished, he turned again and smiled and said "Lee! You're up! Did you sleep at all?"

I told him that I had slept, that I didn't know how long, but I was pretty sure it was more than I had slept at one time in months, and that I was surprised, since I normally took Xanax. "The snow and the motherwort tea," he replied. "A few hours in the cold, finished off with Catherine's motherwort tea, and Xanax is history." His accent was so familiar, and so musical, that it made me want to hear him talk, which was, again, something new for me.

"Where's Ring?" I asked.

Samu looked confused. "With Robert. He's Robert's dog. He'll come to breakfast with Robert."

I paused. Something didn't make sense. "Why did Robert bring him here?"

"Because he's Robert's dog. He goes where Robert goes. And Robert relies on him to help with his anxiety. It's true we don't normally have animals here, but Ring's basically a service dog at this point and it was the only way Robert could come, so we said okay. It's been really nice having him here, actually."

"But…"

Samu stood facing me, silent.

"But, isn't Robert walking the pillars?"

"Yes, that is the plan."

"So he's just leaving Ring here then? Will he stay with you?"

"No," Samu repeated, "Ring is Robert's dog. He'll go with Robert. Robert can't complete the walk without him."

This bothered me in some way I couldn't entirely process, a feeling of discomfort without words or images to go with it, something akin to the feeling of being watched from behind.

"Lee, let me show you how to make your breakfast. You will see, this will be so much easier for you to eat." Samu motioned for me to come and stand at the counter next to him. He pointed at a large waxed cardboard box with pictures of oranges on it, filled with different kinds of greens. And then to a bowl next to it with the ground seeds he'd been measuring.

"So easy, so nutritious. You take handfuls of greens and pack them this way into the blender. Then you use this scoop and pour the flax into one hand til you can't hold any more, and put it on top of the greens like this. Then you come here," and he opened a door at one side of the kitchen, leaned out, and quickly lifted the lid of a chest freezer against the outside wall of the building, "and pick out some fruit, whatever you like, and fill the blender the rest of the way."

He closed the door and walked back to the counter, holding a bag of frozen peaches, which he poured into the blender. "We pick and freeze our own berries when they're in season, but we do buy some things and these are my favorite." He moved over to the sink. "Then you add water and you blend. So easy. Like this." He put the blender back on its stand and turned it on, almost lovingly, then switched it off and looked at the resulting yellowish green liquid, obviously pleased. "So good."

He poured it into two tall metal containers that looked like crosses between coffee cups and water bottles, then fastened lids on and stuck in metal straws. He handed me one of the drinks, and it looked cold and uninviting. I took it and, I guess, looked skeptical.

"Lee," Samu said. "Please. Try a sip."

And I did. It was cold, and slightly sweet, and surprisingly easy to swallow.

"So good," said Samu.

THE GREENHOUSE

The first part of every day, Catherine said, I would spend in the soil greenhouse. I was still unsure how this would help prepare me for my journey. Catherine had told me over the phone that I'd be trained to calm and settle my mind before I'd be allowed to walk, but I hadn't asked many questions about what that entailed. I realized now that I'd expected something like lectures about the Society's philosophy and instructions on how to do the walk properly, maybe having to recite the things they wanted to hear to show I was of sound mind and sufficiently instructed. I'd thought there might also be some sort of meditation, which I could just go through the motions of. Gardening was not something I'd imagined.

But now I followed Catherine out the kitchen side door to a covered walkway leading to three structures. The walkway was short, less than 20 yards, but we'd put on our parkas, hats, and gloves in the kitchen, because the thermometer read -25 degrees Centigrade.

The cold on my face felt bracing, in a way that I appreciated—and it was this second feeling, the appreciation, rather than the cold itself, that made me stop midway. I purposefully and forcefully inhaled through my nose, which stung, and I looked off to the right side. It was dark, and I could barely see a few discernible shapes.

"Meditation and training huts," Catherine said, and waited patiently for me to start walking again. "We'll go there in a few days."

She opened the door to the first greenhouse and ushered me in, then started removing her outer layers. I did the same.

The domed walls were made of plastic with descending pipes in multiple places, and there were paths in every direction between raised beds of wood-framed soil on top of gravel mounds. In the different plots were an array of vegetation—kale, chard, beans, cucumbers, several varieties of squash, and some things I didn't recognize.

"The soil is the first element, the skin of God," said Catherine, crouching by the nearest plot and plunging her fingers into the dirt. "We have to use hydroponics here, though, to produce sufficient quantity, but soil is necessary for life. It contains the minerals, bacteria, fungi—the *life*—that the plants need, that we need. Touching it, breathing it in, getting it in our mouths, is necessary not only for physical health but for spiritual connection. We discharge unhealthy electrical currents into the soil. It's the great stabilizer, the source of all equanimity. That's why we start here. We work from the outside in."

She motioned for me to squat next to her and do as she did, so I dug my fingers into the soil. It was soft and felt aerated, almost fluffy, on the top, and more solid and compacted the farther down I pushed. "Don't be afraid of it," she continued. "Soil is not dirty. Soil is the cleanest thing we have. Soil will not hurt you."

"I'm not worried about getting hurt, Catherine." I looked at her. "That's why I'm here."

"I know," she nodded. "But people sometimes maintain aversions even in crisis. I need you to look at the soil as your respite, your sanctuary. I want you to ground the painful energy going through you by touching it, really feeling it grain by grain on your hands. I want you to breathe deeply while you work in here, to never look at what you're doing as a task to be gotten through, but rather as your relief. Why you are here."

She then showed me where the tools were stored and how to use them, and wrote on a white board what I was to do in each bed. I'd start each day with a blank board, which she would fill with instructions, and when I was finished doing everything listed, I would erase it all, but not check off or cross out any item before that. In between, I would work as my body allowed, resting on the ground whenever I needed to. I would not push myself, but I would devote myself. And when I was finished, I would erase.

Sunrise

I'd been working with the plants for what felt like a couple of hours, though I had no reason to check the time. I had squatted and weeded, bent over a soil mixer, harvested kale, and finally lay down on the ground, which was much colder than the air, and closed my eyes. When I opened them, the sun was rising.

Through the plastic, it looked like a gradually intensifying glow, first red and then gold. I remembered the northern lights and wondered what they'd look like from this vantage point, through the cloud of the plastic walls and roof. I tried to forget where I was, and what I was, and just watch the colors change. I looked at my fingers, coated in a thin layer of dirt, and watched the inside light slowly overcome by the light from outside.

When the sun was fully risen, I erased the white board, picked up the box of cut kale, and went back to the kitchen, where Samu asked me how it went and handed me another glass of the green-gold liquid he'd made earlier.

"That is the first pillar, Lee," Samu said. "The connection of your skin to the earth. Not just the skin on your hands, but the lining of your lungs, your nose, your mouth. Doing this every day will help you feel, understand, and accept this layer of yourself. It's where we start."

"Catherine called the soil the first element," I said. "You just called it the first pillar. I thought the pillars were real structures, in the snow, that we walk to."

"They are. Those are pillars too. But they're based on the pillars of our philosophy. Each pillar on the trail represents a philosophical pillar, and each philosophical pillar is about an element of God."

Samu's God talk reminded me of childhood Sundays with my mother, and the synagogue services Rachel had to attend while preparing for her Bat Mitzvah. In both contexts, I would look around at the other people in the congregation, faces buried in prayer books or lifted toward the pastor or rabbi or staring blankly ahead or out the window, and wonder if any of them really had the sense that an omnipotent being was looking down at them, if there was a single person in the room who in truth felt anything beyond the need to get through the hour quietly and without too much shifting in their seats.

To be fair, Samu's description of God was a far cry from the old man in the sky I'd been raised on and that Rachel had played along with in order to get through her ceremony. But talking about God still seemed to me like a pretend activity, something one did in childhood in order to complete an expected task—get confirmed or Bat Mitzvahed—and then move on to adult things. I supposed being at the sanctuary wasn't all that different; I was trying to complete a task and move on. I didn't really have to believe anything in order to do that. So I nodded at Samu and focused on drinking the blended vegetables and fruit.

As I did, I became aware of an earthy taste I hadn't noticed earlier in the day. I almost thought I could taste the soil in the liquid. After the hours spent in the greenhouse, the drink's cool sweetness felt welcome in a way that nothing I'd taken in had felt in months. I finished and, without asking, Samu refilled my glass. To my relief, no one offered, or asked me to eat, anything solid.

"Samu, I need to lie down for a while. I'm trying to stay focused but I just need a break."

"That is fine. It's a little after nine. Just go lie down for as long as you need. When you are ready, go to the main room and I will meet you there. The next thing to start on is yoga."

I had turned to head back to my room but stopped in my tracks when Samu mentioned yoga. "Yoga? I don't think I can do yoga. No one told me I'd have to. I really don't have the energy."

"Lee, please do not worry. This is very gentle. There are energies stored in your body that need to be released and this is one way to do it. It's not for exercise, I promise you. Did you know that yoga was developed to help with meditation? Not for exercise. Are you surprised? It was to calm the body enough for the yogis to be able to sit in meditation. So to get ready for meditation, you must start doing some gentle yoga. If we start you on meditation now, you will have trouble. It will not work well and you will be frustrated. So we start with the soil and the yoga. Eventually, those will help you meditate. We take one step at a time, okay? Please, if you are full, go lie down. Then, when you are up and ready, go to the lodge and we will start."

Back in my room, I lay on the bed in a fetal position, curling around the hollow ache in my chest. Closing my eyes, I felt Rachel lying in the curve of my body, between my arms, the way she did as a child. This was something I had not felt in the months since her death, and though it was disarming, I wanted it to continue.

Some time later, I realized I'd been asleep. The first thing I noticed when I opened my eyes was the thin layer of dirt still crusted on my fingers.

RING

When I got to the lodge, the fire wasn't burning. I remembered Catherine telling me that, in the dark hours, she liked to burn logs for comfort but that the building was mostly heated by geothermal and solar. The room felt chillier than last night but still relatively comfortable and the windows, while small, were numerous enough to make it bright and inviting.

Robert was there, cleaning the floor with some kind of Swiffer mop. Ring, lying on one of the couches, was watching him. I nodded to both of them and sat down on a chair across from Ring. He jumped off the couch, came to sit by my legs, pressed against me with his back, and yawned. I absentmindedly put my hand on him, and he turned his head and licked it.

When Robert was done cleaning the floor, he walked over slowly, a slight smile on his face. I surprised myself when I spoke.

"Samu said you're taking Ring when you walk the pillars."

Robert nodded.

"Is he sick too?"

Robert was silent for a moment, his smile gone.

"No, he's not sick."

I sat, trying to figure out what it was that I wanted to ask or say. Nothing came to me. I looked at the floor.

"He's nine years old and I've had him since he was a puppy. Since then, it's just been the two of us. I can't do it without him. I'm like an Egyptian pharaoh; I need my dog with me when I go. Together forever." He smiled weakly. "Besides, he doesn't have anywhere else to go."

This shocked me, but I nodded, trying to suppress the feeling rising up in me.

"Would Catherine and Samu let him stay here?"

Robert shook his head, looking slightly irritated.

I replied, too quickly, "I just thought, since he's not sick..."

Robert looked at me carefully. "Lee," he said. "Are *you* sick?"

I didn't answer, just continued looking at the floor, while Robert called to Ring and they both left the room.

YOGA

Waiting for Samu, I thought of Susan for the first time in days. She didn't know where I was. I had thought of texting her before my cell phone became useless, but decided it would be harder for her later if we continued communicating. Now I wasn't sure I had thought that through clearly. There was no cell service here, no internet. If I wanted to contact her, I'd have to ask to use the satellite phone and call her, hear her voice. The thought made the aching spot in my chest run cold like ice water. It seemed best not to think about it, not to think about her.

When Samu came in, I almost laughed, despite myself. He was wearing bright red stretch pants and looked a bit like Pa in the illustrated *Night Before Christmas* that I used to read to Rachel. Minus the sleep cap.

"We are here!" he exclaimed, smiling. "Today just you and me. When you are comfortable with the routine, you will join Robert and Viviana."

Samu disappeared into the passageway and quickly returned with two yoga mats, one orange and one green, and unfurled them on the wood floor between the ring of seats and the inactive wood stove.

"You have never done yoga?" he asked.

"I took a few classes years ago. But it's been a long time. And I don't have much energy."

"Energy is life force. Your life force is dim. Yoga doesn't take energy away from you, it moves and focuses it and releases what needs to be released. This is the second pillar, energy, chi. Yoga is one way to feel that. Certain movements also move your lymph in your body, which is so important.

You are here to get clarity and stillness and reach all the layers of yourself. Especially if you are going to walk. You cannot just focus on the mind and make believe the body is separate and just carrying your head around for you. Your mind runs on chemicals that come from other parts of your body. How those chemicals form and move is important to your clarity and your connection to God."

While he spoke, he lay down on his back on the orange mat and motioned for me to do the same on the green one. "We will start by learning how to breathe. Did you know that breathing is yoga? Breathing is also pranayama, which we will do another time, but it is yoga too. Put your hands on your belly like this, right below your belly button. Yes, like that. When you breathe in, breathe into the space below your hands so your hands go up like an elevator. To a count of four—1, 2, 3, 4—and out four, and your hands should ride the elevator down like this. Yes? Good, Lee. That is so good."

We breathed like that for so long that I lost all sense of time, and at some point felt almost in a dream state, with my breath, with Samu's breath, with sensing my stomach as the locus of my breath rather than something I was obligated to fill. Sometimes thoughts entered my mind, but I was so tired, and the breathing felt so safe, so comforting, that I allowed myself to be engulfed in it.

When Samu spoke again, I was startled.

"Okay, Lee, that is so good. Now we learn sun salutations. This is what will move your lymph. You will see. So good."

DINNER

When I arrived in the kitchen, Viviana was the only one there.

"Hello," Viviana said, with a serious expression but gentle eyes. "We're cooking tonight. Catherine and Samu are doing some intensive work with Robert since he's in his last weeks, so I said I'd show you the ropes. How's your first day been?"

"Has it only been one day?" I asked, partly seriously.

"I know, it's tiring at first. You'll feel less and less tired as the days go on. Everybody seems to. Even Robert, with everything he's dealing with."

I wanted to ask Viviana what pronoun to use, and to offer mine, though it all seemed somewhat beside the point. Maybe whatever part of me shut down the day we got the call about Rachel had taken my pronouns with it.

I also wanted to ask Viviana what brought her or them to this place, as I couldn't see any sign of physical illness. But I didn't want to have to answer the question myself. So I responded about Robert instead.

"Robert told me he's taking Ring with him when he walks the pillars," I said.

Viviana looked at me, with an expression that was a cross between amusement and suspicion. "Yeah, that's what he told me too."

"Doesn't it seem strange to you, when there's nothing wrong with Ring?" I asked.

"I don't know about you, Lee, but things stopped seeming strange to me a long time ago. About the time I decided to fly to a sanctuary out in the snow and never go home again. I figure if that's okay with me, probably most other things are gonna be okay with me too. That and it's not my business." Viviana looked straight into my eyes. I wasn't used to that anymore, and broke the gaze by looking at the floor.

I asked what I could do to help with dinner.

"Someone soaked lentils, so I guess we're having lentils," Viviana said. "I was thinking maybe a dahl. We need some vegetables too. You wanna go in the cooler there and see what's been harvested and pick out some things that look good?"

I did as Viviana requested, and brought back some broccoli and a small box of spinach, as well as a few tomatoes that must have come from one of the hydroponic greenhouses. Viviana smiled approvingly.

"How long have you been here?" I asked.

"Got here a couple weeks before you. Feels like longer."

"When are you walking the pillars?"

"Don't know yet. Don't even know if I am walking them. Just taking it day by day and trying to learn. Purifying myself, you know? Stillness and all that. Moving energy out of me that isn't mine. Trying to find the part that is." At that, all mirth left Viviana's face.

I nodded. "I'll cook the vegetables," I said.

SLEEP

At dinner, Robert looked tired and pensive. Catherine and Viviana talked about the next day's work in the greenhouse and the schedule for something called EFT. Ring lay under the table again, pressed against my legs. At one point, I absentmindedly handed him a piece of broccoli, which he took politely between his teeth and then swallowed whole.

Samu smiled at me. I tried to smile back but knew it was half-hearted and unconvincing. I picked at my food, wishing I could get away with having another blended drink instead, but aware I had promised to eat. With effort, I filled my spoon with dahl and rice and put it in my mouth, saving myself the obligation of talking.

It was only about four p.m., but it was getting dark, and I was tired from the gardening and the yoga. When I finished, I said quietly that I needed to go to bed.

"We'll make a fire in the wood stove after dinner and you're welcome to join us. It's so good to sit by the fire after dinner." Samu smiled broadly.

"I think I just need to lie down. I'm sorry. But thank you."

Robert looked up from his food and met my eye for a moment, then looked down at his plate again.

Back in my room, I climbed onto the bed without removing my clothes and lay on top of the sheet and blanket. Unable to even think, I was only aware of the ache in my chest and wanting to be asleep.

I made a mental note to ask tomorrow about seeing the northern lights. If they beckoned to me on the train, I wanted to know what they would say to me now that I was here.

When I woke up, it was still dark, but that told me little about the time of night or day. I listened for sounds outside my door in the hallway and heard none. I reached for my cell phone: 3:35. Disappointed at first that it was too early to get up, I realized with surprise that I must have slept more than ten hours straight. I didn't remember any dreams. I was still in my clothes.

Normally each time I woke was the same. A moment remembering a dream of Rachel as if it were real, then realizing it had been a dream and I was not really there, then suddenly remembering she was gone and the pain becoming unbearable in my chest. In the apartment, I sometimes responded by taking another Xanax to try to get back to sleep, but then I'd usually only slept two or three hours. Here I had slept more than a full night's worth and I had no Xanax. I had awakened and known where I was and why, so there was no shock.

My legs started to get restless and I wondered what to do. As I shifted in bed, my skin felt clammy under my clothes and I tried to remember the last time I'd washed. No one had tried to get me to bathe since arriving, for which I was grateful. In fact, I hadn't seen the shower, though I was told it was heated with geothermal power and was in a different place than the bathroom, which had a composting toilet and a sink that ran only cold water at a trickle. There were no bathtubs here, water being difficult to pipe in and heat and thus used sparingly.

With all the emphasis on purification, no one seemed focused on washing. I wondered how many more days I could get through before Catherine or Samu said something. As uncomfortable as the clamminess felt, I had no interest in starting this morning, or any morning, with finding the shower or getting in it. But I didn't have any sense of what to do instead, knowing I had a couple of hours before it would be time to get up and not wanting to be alone with my thoughts.

Without really deciding, I found myself stretching out on my back, putting my hands on my stomach, and breathing into my belly to raise them slowly up and down the way Samu had taught me. After a while, I drifted back to sleep.

DAY TWO

With my blended drink in hand, I entered the greenhouse and looked at the white board. It was still empty. Unsure what to do, I took off my parka, hat, and gloves and went to the bed of kale. Squatting, I dug my fingers into the soil the way Catherine had shown me to do the day before, and breathed. I felt the ache in my chest run cold with anxiety, so I stopped and hugged my knees and buried my face in them.

When I heard the door close, I looked up. Catherine was taking off her parka and watching me.

"I put my fingers in the soil and breathed like you showed me, but it made me anxious so I stopped." I looked at her.

"Lee, the soil didn't make you anxious. Neither did the breathing. You just got still enough to feel what's there all the time."

That did not feel like a helpful thing to say. I did not want to feel this all the time.

"The best thing to do when that happens is to let yourself feel it and to keep breathing, and keep focusing on feeling the soil on the skin of your hands. If you react in fear by pushing it away, that's why it stays. It's just energy. You need to let it move through you."

"It doesn't feel like energy. And it doesn't feel like it will move through me. It feels like I need to get away from it."

"Please trust me. I'll do it with you." She came over, put her hands in the soil, and motioned to me with her head. I squatted next to her and did the same. "Now breathe with me," she said, "and stay aware of the anxiety. You don't need to focus on it, just stay aware of it, and tell it in your mind that you see it, and that you want to take care of it, and it should let you know what it needs."

"The anxiety?" I asked.

"The anxiety. Do that, and then stay aware of it, almost with your inner peripheral vision if that makes sense, and then focus on your deep breathing and the feel of the soil on your hands. Like this."

And we squatted there, breathing with our stomachs and feeling the soil. I closed my eyes and did what she said to do, and felt it welling up inside me. Just at that moment, Catherine said, "Don't run from it, Lee. Let it be. I promise you it will move through you." So I stayed, feeling with fear that something was coming, like a train, to run me down, but that it was coming from somewhere inside my chest. I let it come, and I breathed, and I felt my hands. And then suddenly it dissipated.

"Oh my god, it went away," I said, rocking back into a sitting position. "I mean, not entirely, but you were right, it kind of passed through me, and now only part of it's there, the part I normally feel, which is like a dull ache."

"Remember that," said Catherine, smiling. "I'll be telling you a lot more things you won't like, but please remember that you have a reason to trust me now."

I considered this and studied Catherine.

"How did you learn this stuff?" I asked artlessly.

"From the Society." She was so matter-of-fact, as if that explained everything.

"Did you start this place?"

"Sort of. It was already in the planning stages when I joined the Society, but I helped get it going and Samu and I are the only ones to run it so far. I was an oncology nurse in Winnipeg at the time, and I was really disheartened by the options available to my patients when they were dying. Another nurse invited me to a class one night at the Society's office, and that was it for me. I realized the Society, and the idea for this sanctuary, were what I'd been looking for. I got more and more involved, ended up on the board, and a few years later, I quit my job and moved here."

With that, she got up and went to the white board to write the instructions for the day.

"Catherine," I asked. "Is the aurora visible from here?"

"From the greenhouse?"

"No, from the property. I was just wondering."

"Yes, it's often visible. Let me know anytime you want to see it after dinner, and I'll go out with you. Eventually, it will become part of your routine, sitting with the aurora. It's just not what we start with, especially because it's not always visible."

"What's wrong with Viviana?" I inquired, kind of abruptly.

"What's wrong with her?" Catherine raised her eyebrows. So, then, Viviana went by her.

"Why is she here. Robert said he has pancreatic cancer. Why is Viviana here?" I realized that maybe I should have asked Viviana herself instead of asking Catherine. But I couldn't imagine doing so.

Catherine came and sat down next to me. "Viviana experienced a rape. She was injured… in a number of ways. She was using conventional therapies and recently gave up on them. So she's in training with us."

"Was she in the military?" I asked, not knowing the outer limits of the information I could request.

"Yes, she was. That's where she was attacked." Catherine looked at me with an open expression, waiting to see if I had any more questions.

I remembered reading about the seventeen-year-old Dutch girl who'd gotten permission to be legally euthanized when she couldn't recover from a childhood rape. I felt slightly nauseous. I didn't want to know any more about what had happened to Viviana.

"Do she and Robert know why I'm here?" I asked instead, trying to change the subject.

"Yes, they know, and you'll get basic information about the next devotee before they arrive. We've tried this different ways, and this is what seems to work best, so we can treat each other with some basic understanding, know when someone has physical limitations or there are things that might particularly scare them. Viviana knew I would tell you at some point. I'm not betraying her. In fact, it's important that you know not to touch her unless she initiates it."

I let that sink in for a moment before changing the subject.

"What about Ring?" I asked. "Why does Ring need to walk the pillars? Can't he stay here instead?"

Catherine looked at me blankly, so I continued. "There's nothing wrong with him and Robert said he's nine so he could have years left."

"Ring doesn't like being separated from Robert. When Robert first got here and tried to leave him in his room, even for short periods, he whined like crazy until we let him out and he got back to Robert. He's gotten better about separating for small amounts of time, but they're still almost always together."

"But Ring doesn't know what the pillars are. You say choice and clarity with the decision is such a big part of walking the pillars. Doesn't it matter that Ring isn't making the choice?"

Catherine looked down. When she looked up, her expression was hard to read but serious. "Lee, I think you need to ask yourself why this concerns you. I'm not being curt. But you decided, in coming here, that you were ready to focus inward and that you don't have much use anymore for the rest of the world. In retreating here, in wanting to walk the pillars, you yourself have made some choices for other people."

I opened my mouth to object to the comparison.

"No, let me finish," she said quickly, raising one hand to gesture me to stop. "Whether you recognize it or not, you're certainly making some choices for the people in your life by removing yourself from them this way, and if you have this much concern about what Robert and Ring are doing, I think you need to think about why that is, and whether you're ready to be here. That's not a judgment or a scolding. It's a real question that I want you to think about."

With that, she stood and put her hand on my shoulder for a moment before going back to the white board, writing the last of the instructions, putting on her parka and gloves, and leaving the building.

SNOW

I hadn't been out in the snow since arriving. I'd seen the snow and walked past it under the covered walkway to the greenhouse, but that was it. I really wanted to be out in it. Really, more than anything, I wanted to freeze. I wanted to feel the snow on my skin. Unless I wanted to deal with frostbite, though, there would not be much touching of snow at this temperature before I was allowed to walk the pillars.

After I was done in the greenhouse and had erased the day's instructions, I realized that I was thirsty and wanted more blended drink. I went to the kitchen and found it empty. For the first time, I followed Samu's instructions and made my own, poured it into a large metal cup, and drank. I was worried it wouldn't taste as good as Samu's, but it did.

I made my way to the lodge to join Robert and Viviana for yoga. But when I got to the large open room, it too was empty, and I felt the overwhelming need to lie down. I climbed onto one of the couches and stretched out, my arm hanging off the side, and closed my eyes. I must have fallen asleep, because after what seemed like only moments, I started at the feeling of something warm and rough on my hand. It was Ring, licking my knuckles and looking at me.

"Hi, Ring," I said, putting my hand on his head. "Are you here to do yoga too?"

I sat up and saw Viviana and Robert laying out their mats, and a third rolled mat on the floor near them. I walked over and unfurled it.

"If I can keep my eyes open long enough, I'm thinking of trying to see the aurora after dinner tonight," I offered. "Have either of you had any luck seeing it?"

"I just started a nightly watch for it as part of my meditation practice," answered Viviana. "I know you haven't learned that yet, but you're welcome to join me."

I thanked her and said I wanted to. Robert demurred. "Ring might want to go, though," Robert said, eying me. "He's been missing the aurora watch since I stopped doing it. If you want to take him out with you, he's pretty well behaved." I stared at Robert for a second, confused as to how a dog who couldn't live without him would be fine leaving him in the lodge and joining us outside. I'd met dogs with separation anxiety, who would be destructive or inconsolable when left in unfamiliar situations, and Ring didn't strike me as anything like them. I started to wonder if Robert was projecting his own anxieties onto Ring. I decided to find out.

"OK," I said. "I'd like that." And I realized, to my surprise, that I would.

HEAT AND COLD

Catherine said she wanted me to take a shower. I knew it was bound to come up at some point, but the way she raised it, and the reasons, were unexpected.

She wanted me to sit in a sauna, and then to rinse with freezing cold water, then to shower in warm water, then to rinse again in cold water. Something about clearing toxins and gathering my life force. It was, she said, one of the steps.

Bath towel in hand, Catherine led me to the last room at the end of the hall where my bedroom was, a room I hadn't been in. There were two differently shaped boxes, each big enough to hold a person, with a chair between them. Catherine put the towel on the chair.

The square box on the left was silver and made of fabric. Inside the box, Catherine explained, was an infrared heating device run on electricity, as well as a seat. She turned it on and set the heat at 130 degrees and the timer to go off after twenty minutes. She explained how to unzip the box and get inside, with my head sticking out, once she left me and I disrobed.

The box on the right was made of white plastic and was the size and shape of a tall refrigerator. Inside was a showerhead and a bar of soap. Catherine showed me how to work the shower, and explained that the bar served both as soap for the body and shampoo for the hair. She explained the cold-warm-cold sequence again, and then left the room, suggesting on her way out that in-between this therapy and cooking dinner, I should rest in my room.

For several minutes after Catherine closed the door, I stood fully dressed, trying to convince myself to start taking off my clothes. The timer was already counting down the minutes I was supposed to be sweating. I realized I could barely remember the last time I had bathed or was naked even for a moment. I had occasionally taken baths in the apartment since Rachel's death, but on heavy doses of Xanax. The few times I changed my clothes each week, I did so one item at a time. I couldn't explain why, exactly, but I had some kind of block against undressing. I'd thought it was just the effort it entailed, and the meaninglessness of it once I didn't have a job to go to or anyone to see. But now I realized it was something else, or at least something more.

I started by removing the pile sweater, and then my pants, leaving me in long underwear and socks. I took each sock off slowly, then pushed the long underwear bottoms down around my feet and stepped out of each leg one at a time. My legs looked thin and spindly in a way I wasn't used to seeing, with rough red blotches around the knees. My toenails were long. I paused, and then removed the long underwear top. I looked down at my scar, where my left breast had been, and at the small sagging breast on the right. This, then, was my body at this point in my life, this end point. This is what it would be now, until it wasn't anything.

Removing my underwear, I unzipped the silver box, got inside, sat down on the seat with my head sticking out of the hole at the top, and zipped it back up. I could feel the heat but did not immediately start sweating. I did, however, immediately wish I could either lie down or had something to occupy me while I sat in the box. Knowing I had to remain sitting there alone, in the silence, in a closed room with no window, inside a box, with my own mind for another twenty minutes, I felt the anxiety rise up inside me again like a freight train coming down the tracks—tracks that I was sitting on, zipped in and unable to move.

My heart started to pound. I realized I was breathing quickly and shallowly, overcome by the awareness of being by myself not only in the room but in a larger sense, trapped in some kind of bubble, a deafening silence without end, a sharp and visceral knowledge that I would never see my daughter again. It was a physical feeling overwhelming me from all sides. I wanted to lie on the floor and hug my knees, but I couldn't do that in the fabric sauna box.

And then I remembered Catherine's instructions. I closed my eyes and slowed my breathing and put my hands on my belly, and in the absence of soil, I put my attention on the heat on my skin, the feeling of air coming in and out of my lungs, and my hands moving with my stomach. And out of the corner of some internal awareness, I watched the anxiety too and let it happen. At first, this seemed like a mistake, and I had the urge to unzip the sauna and go running out to the main room naked and screaming for someone to help me. But this was coming from inside, and all anyone could tell me was to do what I was already doing. I asked the anxiety what it needed. I let it be. If it was going to kill me, so be it. It would save me a lot of work.

And then, just as in the greenhouse, it started to dissipate. And I realized I was sweating. A lot. Sweat was trickling down my stomach and my spine, and a drop was starting to roll down my right leg.

When the timer went off, I unzipped the sauna and got into the shower. I turned on the cold water, and it was really cold. I wasn't sure I could do it. But then I remembered wanting to be in the snow, to feel it on my skin, and I put my arms, and then my stomach and legs, under the stream. Finally, I turned around and stood with my head under the water. It was so cold that I felt breathless. I remembered Catherine telling me that this feeling would last about thirty seconds and then pass if I could stand to stay in the cold that long. I don't think I made it more than ten or fifteen seconds. I stepped out of the water, gasping for air, and made the water warmer.

Back under it, I regained my breath. I took the soap and quickly rubbed it in my hair, which I was surprised to feel reached almost to my shoulders when wet. It had been so short for years, but I hadn't bothered to get it cut since Rachel. Hadn't even thought of it. Didn't look in the mirror. I realized suddenly that I had no idea what I looked like, that my own mental image of myself likely bore little resemblance to what Catherine, Samu, Robert, and Viviana saw when they looked at me.

I also realized that whatever I looked like, it was different than how Rachel knew me, that she had never seen me thin like this or with long hair. I didn't know if I was in fact the same person who had raised her. I couldn't place how this shell I was carrying around related to the parent I'd been, to the person who had held Rachel on my lap, who had buried her.

Again the anxiety rose. I placed my hands against the plastic wall of the shower this time and concentrated on the water running down my skin, the breath in my belly, and my feet on the floor, and I watched the train as it came for me. And again it went through me, and past me, and with a wave of exhaustion, I sat on the plastic shower floor under the warm water. I closed my eyes and put my hands over my ears, the way I had as a child, and listened to what sounded like a rainstorm all around me. I used to love that feeling, that sound. I don't know how long I sat there.

Then I remembered Catherine's admonition about the amount of warm water I should use, and I stood up and turned it to cold again. Again my breath left my lungs. I might have lasted a little longer, but I turned off the shower before I regained my breath.

Stepping out of the shower stall and reaching for the towel, I felt a surge of something in my body, something that was not anxiety. It's hard to explain, but what it felt most like was freedom.

AURORA

After dinner, I went to the main room of the lodge with Viviana, who wanted to sit by the fire for a bit before going out to see the lights. I sat next to her on a couch facing the wood stove's glass door.

"Watch the flames for a while. Don't think about anything. Just watch the flames," Viviana said.

After a few minutes, I felt something like a sigh somewhere in my chest and was suddenly aware of the utter quiet all around me.

"You're right," I said. "It helps."

"Yeah," said Viviana, looking at the stove. "So good, right? *So good.*"

I turned to look at her, and she laughed.

"Sorry," she said. "I guess I still have a little wickedness left in me. Must meditate more!" We both laughed softly.

"Is that some kind of common phrase in Hungarian?" I asked her.

"No idea," she replied, still smiling.

Eventually, Robert came into the room with Ring following close behind. Ring was wearing a little red coat and red paw coverings and looked, frankly, ridiculous.

"He's dressed and ready," Robert offered, "whenever you want to go. I'm gonna sit here. I'm beat."

"Ready?" Viviana asked me. We both started putting on our outer layers as Ring walked over to us and looked up expectantly.

"You know you're going with us?" I asked him, looking down at his face, which had one ear up and one ear down.

"Always," Robert replied for him. "It's hard to pull anything over on him. You know, when he was young, I made a list, like parents do with toddlers, of all the words he knew. Fifty-something. Fifty-something words. Never met another dog like him. I've been told he has some border collie in him and that's where his brains come from."

Ring turned his head back to look at Robert, as if acknowledging this last comment.

"Okay then, genius," said Viviana, patting her hand on the outside of her thigh, "let's go."

The three of us walked out. Halfway down the walkway, we stepped off to the right into the dark and the snow. I couldn't see much, but Viviana knew where the path was and took the lead.

As soon as we were a few feet out onto the path, Ring took off running down it. "Ring!" I shouted, alarmed, and he stopped short, turned, crouched his front end down to the ground with his hind end sticking up in the air, and raced back to us. When he reached me, he stopped long enough for me to put my hand on his back, then jumped into the snow at the side of the path and stuck his head so far into it that all I could see were his torso and legs. Pulling his head back out, he sneezed, did another play bow, and came trotting back to me.

"He's playing!" I said with wonder.

"He's really playful," responded Viviana. "I've seen him do that before. It's pretty funny."

Once Ring seemed satisfied with his romp, we continued walking until we got to a small platform raised off the snow with four stairs leading up to it. In the dark, I couldn't tell what it was made of, but it was big enough for the three of us to lie on. Viviana spread a thin foil blanket over it and motioned for me to climb up. As I put my foot on the first step, Ring pushed past me and bounded up.

There were some stars visible, but the sky must have been cloudy, because there were far fewer than when I'd walked out to the greenhouse in the morning. Viviana sat cross-legged on the foil, and I did the same. She patted her hand on the blanket and Ring came over and sat between us. Viviana then took another foil blanket out of her parka pocket and wrapped it around the three of us.

"In Churchill, they had a hotel with heated glass domes to watch the lights from," I said.

"When were you in Churchill?"

"I went there on my way here. I mean, not really on the way, but that's how I went."

Viviana looked at me as if I had three heads. "Why didn't you just fly from Winnipeg?"

"My daughter and I had planned to take a trip up here, James Bay and Hudson Bay, and she really wanted to go to Churchill. Wanted to see the tundra and the polar bears. So I went. I only stayed a night."

Viviana seemed to accept this as sufficient reason. "So did you do it?" she asked.

"Did I do what?"

"Watch the lights from a heated dome on top of a hotel."

"No."

Viviana was silent for a minute. "Well, this ain't no heated dome," she offered. "But I think that's the point—to really dissolve into the lights when they come, to join them. I don't know if you could do that from underneath a glass dome."

"Exactly what I was thinking," I responded. "I skipped it because I'm a purist." She looked at me questioningly, and I laughed. "Actually, I couldn't get my ass out of bed long enough to do something like that. I've kind of regretted it, so I'm glad this platform is here. I was thinking we'd be standing in the snow craning our necks and waiting for hours."

"We might have to wait for hours. I normally meditate while I'm waiting, and if they come, I lie down and watch them like we watched the flames inside, just breathing and watching. But I know they haven't given you any instruction on that yet. We can talk if you want."

"Okay," I said. "Though I can't promise scintillating conversation. I haven't had a lot to say these last months."

"If I understand anything," said Viviana, "it's that."

We were both silent for a while. Ring sighed loudly and lay down with his head on my knee, under the foil blanket.

"Viviana turned to look at us. "You seem to connect with him. You have a dog?"

"Not since I was young," I answered. "My wife was allergic. Is allergic." I paused for a while, thinking about that, looking up at the sky. "But when I was a kid, I had a dog I was really close to. Daisy. When she died, I locked myself in my room and didn't eat for almost two days. I think I was eleven. We never adopted another dog, and then I met Susan in college and she was allergic. So…"

"I had a dog in the army. Worked with him, anyway. Really smart, like Ring. I have no idea where he is now."

"Do you know if he made it out?"

"Nope."

"How long were you in the army?"

"Sixteen years. Four more and I would have had a pension. Tried to stick it out but it became impossible."

A long time passed without either of us saying anything. It wasn't like talking to someone anywhere else. We both knew there were a lot of "do not touch" signs around each other's necks. Knowing this somehow made it more comfortable, for me anyway. Being out there in the cold, in the dark, in the snow with Viviana sitting silently inches from me, not expecting me to say anything, gave me a sense of calm that was an inexplicably strong relief.

And then the lights came.

DAY THREE

The next morning, I could not get out of bed. Waking in the dark, I felt a weight on my chest, an anvil pushing me down. I had, of course, felt this before.

I tried to talk myself into going to the kitchen for a blended drink, or going straight to the greenhouse. But it was dark, and I was incapable of caring how ungrateful I might seem for refusing to participate today. If that fear could move me, it would have moved me months ago, back in the apartment.

Lying there on the sanctuary bed, I eventually surrendered and waited to fall back asleep. Without the Xanax, though, and having slept a full night, sleep didn't return. I tried to focus on my breathing, but couldn't get myself to concentrate on it for more than a few breaths and gave up.

After what seemed like hours, there was a soft knock on my door. It was Catherine, and I tried to get myself to stand up, but I couldn't. I eventually told her this through the door.

"Can I come in and talk to you?" she asked.

I agreed, and she came in and sat down on the rocking chair.

"Would it help if I bring you your drink in here?" she asked.

I didn't think so.

"I have an idea," she said, without the slightest hint of judgment. "I'll ask Viviana to take your shift in the greenhouse. What if I walk you there and you just lie down on the floor while she works? You don't have to do or say anything. She'll understand. That way you can keep lying down, but you'll breathe in the soil microbes and won't be alone."

I told her I felt bad about Viviana needing to take my shift.

"But it's not a burden. To her or to anyone else. It's part of our practice, and it doesn't matter to her what order she does it in. She'll understand. I promise."

She asked me to try to get dressed while she went to get Viviana, and said she'd be back to walk me to the greenhouse.

Getting dressed meant putting my pile pullover over my long underwear and stepping into my insulated pants. It was all I could do.

When Catherine returned, she gave me her arm. I held it with my hand and leaned on her a little as we walked to the door of my room. I stopped. "My parka…"

"Leave it. You'll be okay on the walkway. It may even help you."

Cold therapy, I thought, remembering the freezing shower. And she was right: When we walked out into the dark of the walkway, the bite of the cold made me inhale sharply, which hurt a little, but it also made me stand up a little straighter and feel more able to make it to the greenhouse on my own. Viviana was inside, taking off her gloves. She looked at me sympathetically.

"I'll be working by the green bean bed," she said. "Come lie down on the ground over there. I won't bother you."

Catherine said she'd bring me a blended drink. I opened my mouth to protest but remembered the agreement and said nothing. I followed Viviana to the green beans and lay down on the floor. Viviana stepped away and returned with a foil blanket.

"You need to put this under you and wrap yourself up in it. Otherwise, you're gonna get cold. Do you want my parka?"

I shook my head but accepted the foil blanket. I lay back and closed my eyes as Viviana returned to working.

Some time later, Catherine was standing over me with a drink.

"I added some turmeric. I'd like you to start putting that in all your drinks. It's an anti-inflammatory and helps with depression. I also added vitamin D. I should have started you on that your first day."

I lifted my head and drank some and lay back down.

"Lee," Catherine said, "I want to do some EFT with you. We'd planned to start that with you in a few days, but I think it'll help now. If you can't sit up, we can do it with you lying down. And if you can't tap, I can do the tapping."

I had no idea what she was talking about, and I neither wanted to sit up nor tap. But the idea of lying there with Catherine tapping on something also seemed a little stranger than I could bear at the moment. So I slowly pushed myself up into a cross-legged position in front of her.

"EFT stands for Emotional Freedom Technique. It's tapping on a set of acupuncture points on your face and torso while tuning in to how you're feeling. It moves energy. What you're feeling right now is stuck energy—a whole lot of stuck energy. It needs to move."

It didn't feel like energy. It felt like lead weights. Kind of the opposite of energy.

But Catherine proceeded to show me all the tapping points on her own face and body, starting with a spot at the inside corner of one of her eyebrows.

She had me trace the points with her.

"You don't need to try to remember any of this right now. Just do what I do and say what I say. But first, what does it feel like in your body? Tell me what it feels like. It's okay if it's just a few words."

"I really don't want to talk. Susan tried to get me to do talk therapy, but I knew it wouldn't help." I didn't see any reason to put myself through that.

"This isn't talk therapy. I promise." Catherine squinted a little while she said this, like she shared my feelings about it. "What really helps with emotional distress isn't talking about it over and over. What helps is learning how to release it from your body. And learning how to actually be in your body, to feel what's happening in it, to be present with it. That's what helps you heal. So just tell me what your body feels like, not what you're thinking, just what your body feels like, physically."

"Heavy," I said. "Like lead weights on me, and inside my chest. Aching in my chest. No energy. I just want to lie down. I…"

Catherine sat patiently and didn't say anything. She waited.

"I want to die."

She nodded. "That's okay," she said. "It's okay to feel that."

Then she asked me to start tapping with the fingertips of my right hand on the outside bone of my left hand, which she called the karate chop point. Over and over, just tapping.

"This is where we start," she said. "It's called the set-up. It's different than the rest of the tapping. Don't think about it. Just repeat after me: 'Even though I feel covered in lead weights.'"

"Even though I feel covered in lead weights."

"And have a terrible ache in my chest.'"

"And have a terrible ache in my chest."

"And I want to die."

I swallowed and paused, then repeated, "And I want to die."

"I accept this is how I'm feeling and I love and honor myself anyway."

I opened my mouth but nothing came out.

"Try," Catherine said.

"I accept this is how I'm feeling and I love and honor myself anyway."

"Even though," she continued.

"Even though."

"I feel I'm at the end of the line and I can't go any further."

"I feel I'm at the end of the line and I can't go any further."

"And I don't even want to get off the ground."

"And I don't even want to get off the ground."

"I love, honor, and accept myself anyway."

"I love, honor, and accept myself anyway."

We'd fallen into a rhythm with Catherine speaking slowly and me repeating her words. "Even though it seems like this feeling will never end," she intoned.

"Even though it seems like this feeling will never end."

"And it feels so heavy and painful in my chest."

"And it feels so heavy and painful my chest."

"I choose to accept this is how I am right now and love myself anyway."

"I choose to accept this is how I am right now and love myself anyway."

She started tapping the point at the corner of her brow, and I copied her, moving among the points as she did.

"This heaviness.'"

"This heaviness."

"Like lead weights."

"Like lead weights."

"The ache in my chest."

"The ache in my chest."

"I don't think I can bear it."

"I don't think I can bear it," I repeated, struck by how she seemed to read my mind, speaking my thoughts for me to repeat back to her.

"I don't think it will ever change."

"I don't think it will ever change."

On and on it went, Catherine saying these phrases and tapping her face, her chest, the top of her head, and me following along. I started to feel a sense of calm and then, all of a sudden, the freight train was coming toward me again. But it was different this time. It wasn't anxiety. It was pain—physical pain in my chest, pain in my head. I wailed, suddenly, and started sobbing. I covered my face.

"No, don't cover your face," Catherine said. "Keep going. Lee, look at me. Keep crying but keep tapping while you cry. You don't need to say anything. Just feel whatever you're feeling—don't push it down—and tap on the points. Trust me. It's like the anxiety. This is energy. It's been stuck in you for a long time. You need to let it move through you. Please. Take your hands off your face and tap. It doesn't matter if I see you crying. It's just energy. It needs to move. You're releasing cortisol through your tears. They need to come out. Don't try to stop them."

I did as she said, but I was crying so hard I could barely get air into my lungs. My face was twisted up terribly and it was all I could do to find the points with my fingers. I couldn't see Catherine's face, so she just kept repeating the places to tap, over and over.

"Corner of the brow. Side of the eye. Under the eye. Under the nose. Chin. Collarbone. Under the arm…"

I don't know how long this lasted. I was inside some kind of storm, like sitting in the shower with my hands over my ears, but the storm was also inside me. It *was* me. I tapped when I could, alternatingly tapping on the points and covering my face and wailing. Eventually, I lost track of where I was and who I was with. There was just the sobbing and sometimes the points, and Catherine repeating the words over and over.

And then, just as suddenly, it stopped. I was shaking, but I was no longer crying. I felt something emanating off me like steam. I was tired, but the heaviness was gone. I felt exhausted but light.

"Take a deep breath," Catherine said. And then, after a pause, she continued.

"One more round. Corner of the brow. I feel a little lighter. Side of the eye. I still have the heaviness but it's less. Under the eye. The heaviness is moving though me. Under the nose…"

ROBERT

That night, when Robert came to dinner, the skin on his face looked more yellow. I hadn't seen him all day. He seemed clammy, with an oily-looking sweat on his forehead and hands. Ring anxiously pressed against his legs as he sat down and did not come over to me.

"I'm not sure I can eat," Robert said to Samu. "I'm pretty nauseous."

"I'll make you some ginger tea," said Samu. "Try eating some white rice and see how you do. Just the rice and tea."

Samu got up and went to the kitchen. I looked at Viviana, who was looking at her plate, and then at Catherine, who was looking at Robert.

"My back hurts too," he told Catherine. "I think I need to move it up. If I wait another ten days, I won't be able to do it."

Catherine nodded. "It's okay. I think you're ready. We can start the last steps tomorrow, and aim for Thursday. Three days. Does that sound right?"

Robert nodded, looking pensive.

Samu returned with the tea. "Ginger tea is so good for nausea," he said, handing the mug to Robert. Robert took a small sip.

Samu sat back down next to Robert and spooned some rice onto his plate. Robert sat for a while before picking up his fork. No one said anything.

After a minute or two, Catherine turned to me and Viviana. "Day after tomorrow, your schedules will be different. There are some things we all need to do to help Robert get ready. It's important to be as calm as possible, so I'd like you both to do heat and cold therapy first thing Wednesday morning, followed by yoga. Then we'll all meditate together. Lee, I'll give you some meditation instruction tomorrow."

I wanted to call Ring over to me and sneak food to him under the table. Then again, I didn't want to see Ring. I was afraid to see him. I felt a coldness in my stomach as if I'd swallowed snow.

I wanted to ask again about whether Ring really needed to go. But looking at Robert, the desire to do so slowly slid away.

DAY FOUR

So I was going to start meditation early. Not early in the day, but early in my stay. Because Robert's last day at the lodge was to be an intensive multi-hour group meditation. Catherine said we all needed to meditate with Robert in order to contribute our energy to the field, to allow him to go deeper. And because our well-wishing, a part of our meditation in which we would focus our good will and inner attention on Robert's well-being, would help him on his journey.

As a result, my greenhouse practice was suspended for two days. My morning started with heat and cold therapy, then yoga with Viviana, and then, after a period of rest, I met Catherine in the meditation hut in the courtyard.

In the daylight, the hut resembled a cross between an igloo and a bread oven. Made out of stone and dome-shaped, it contained only narrow, horizontal, sliver-like windows in a band around the dome about two-thirds of the way up.

When I entered, the interior seemed dark until my eyes adjusted. There was no furniture, only thick overlapping red rugs that seemed woven out of something like burlap or jute, supporting several bright red and blue cushions. The heat felt like it was coming from the floor. Which solar or radiant mechanism controlled that, I couldn't tell.

On small projections of stone jutting out from the walls at varying heights were candles and smoldering incense sticks. The smell was viscerally familiar in a way I couldn't place.

Catherine was sitting on a cushion in the center of the floor and smiled at me, motioning me to sit on another cushion facing her, which I did.

She explained that we were going to do a bit of accelerated meditation instruction so that I could participate in Robert's send-off session the next day, but that it would only be reasonable to expect me to participate for thirty to sixty minutes. Robert, Catherine, and Samu would meditate the entire day, breaking only to drink blended drinks. Viviana would participate as much as she was able, perhaps two to three hours. Catherine was going to teach me the meditation method now, and I would practice it on my own in my room tonight and then join them here in the morning for a portion of the next day's meditation.

Catherine showed me how to sit and how to hold my hands, and then told me to close my eyes and breathe from my belly the way Samu had taught me in yoga, but in an upright sitting position. She instructed me to be aware of the sensation of the air moving into and out of my nostrils. When she said that, I noticed, probably for the first time in my life, that breathing through my nose created a slight burning sensation on the skin inside my nostrils.

When I was comfortable with this and settling into myself, Catherine introduced the mantra, *So Ham*, explaining that it means "I am that" in Sanskrit. "It's a recognition of the divine and that we are part of the divine. This is one of the last pillars. Robert's been meditating on this mantra for over a month. When we meditate with it tomorrow, the feeling that we're all connected strands in the web of the divine will be palpable. This is what will carry Robert on his journey, what will help him truly go home."

She taught me how to focus on the mantra internally, to reintroduce it quietly in my mind whenever I noticed other thoughts arising. And for this particular meditation, when I became aware of a thought, I would turn my inner attention to Robert and send him good will before reintroducing the mantra and continuing on.

We practiced in this way for thirty minutes or so. Every so often, in progressively lengthening intervals, Catherine would ring a small bell and invite me to open my eyes and then ask if I had any questions.

When we finished, Catherine joined her hands and put them to her heart, bowed her head, and said, "Namaste. Do you know what that means?"

I shook my head no.

"It means the light in me recognizes the light in you. It's the way we end the *So Ham* meditation."

I repeated the gesture and moved to get up.

"Sit a moment," she said quietly. So I settled back onto my cushion.

"Robert and Samu and I will be meditating all day tomorrow, as I said. There's the question of Ring."

"The question of him walking the pillars?" I asked hopefully.

"No, the question of what he'll do while Robert meditates. Robert sometimes brings him here, but it can be distracting. Lately, he's taken to leaving him with me or Samu for the longer meditation periods, or in his room. But tomorrow will be a very long day for that, and we won't be available to help. I was hoping you'd take Ring for the afternoon and early evening. You seem to enjoy being with him."

The icy feeling returned to the pit of my stomach.

"I don't know. It's really hard for me to think about him being taken on the pillar walk, that he only has a few days left to live. I'm not sure I can handle spending that much time with him, knowing that."

Catherine pondered this for a few seconds before responding. "Lee, if I'm not mistaken, you're still planning on walking when you're ready. You don't know when that will be. You don't know how long Ring would have without walking, or if he will even be here tomorrow. None of us know. Your own time may be very limited. According to what you've expressed, you want it to be very limited."

She spoke gently but deliberately, her eyes soft but her mouth set firmly whenever she paused. "Being ready for anyone's departure, including your own, means being able to experience the day for what it is, the hours for what they are, the moments for what they are. To be present in them. Ring's death is just an idea right now. Tomorrow, it will likely be just an idea as well. Your idea, not his. Tomorrow, he'll be lonely and restless while Robert meditates. Tomorrow, he'll be happier with your company. And if you can let go of the death that you've created for him in your mind, a death that hasn't happened yet, that might not ever happen the way you imagine it, and see him as alive tomorrow if he is alive tomorrow—if you can do that, it will open your heart and calm your mind. And bring you closer to your own readiness."

"I don't think my heart needs opening, Catherine. My heart's been open."

"Your heart *was* open. I agree with you about that. I don't agree that it's open now. You've retreated so far into yourself that even you don't know where you've gone. Please, try this with Ring tomorrow. Treat it as a meditation. Focus on him, his breathing, his movements, the sounds he makes as he walks or breathes or sleeps. When you sense a thought arising, either about your own conception of his future or anything else, gently reintroduce the practice of paying attention to him. To him. Not to your fears about him."

I bowed my head and made a slight nodding motion. She was right. I felt fear.

"And what about the feeling of fear?" I asked. "In my chest. What do I do with that?"

"You acknowledge it. You notice it, you acknowledge it, and you place your attention on Ring. Do not fight the fear. Invite it to tell you what it needs. Invite it to co-exist with you. And then simply put your attention elsewhere, retaining some peripheral awareness of it like you've done with anxiety. Because it's the same thing. It's all fear. And none of it has to do with the moment you're in, the moment that's passing. All of it has to do with your mental expectations, your memories, your uncertainty about the future. There's a wonderful Mark Twain quote: 'I've lived through some terrible things in my life, some of which actually happened.' You've lived through some terrible things, Lee. None of them are happening today. Don't live through Ring's death while he's still alive in the lodge, and happy, and wants to spend time with you tomorrow. You have no idea what's going to happen after that."

I nodded again, and we stood up to leave.

"Lee," she added, "Robert's also planning to walk. Ring's going with him. But you haven't protested spending time these next two days helping Robert. You realize that the time you spend is to help. It's only Ring you feel fear about."

I thought about that.

"Robert's sick," I said. "And it's his choice."

"Those thoughts are parts of a complicated value system in your mind. The experience will be harder for Robert because he's sick, because he knows what he's doing. And yet you can offer him your time and attention without being overwhelmed by fear or grief."

"I guess that's because I understand why he's doing it himself. I want to do it too. And I want his last days to be as easy as possible, and for him to reach what he wants to reach. None of that applies to Ring. He seems healthy. He seems to want to be alive. No one's asked him."

"Just as no one asked you before taking Rachel's life. Whatever happened to Rachel, you were left here. It wasn't your choice. You're unhappy about it, because you find it unbearable to be left without her. Yet you have no fear for Ring if Robert doesn't take him. Being left here might not be Ring's choice either. He doesn't want Robert to leave him. You see how intense their relationship is, the way Robert is his touchstone. You don't want to be left here with grief, without a place that feels like home. Yet you've decided that's what Ring would choose if he could."

I opened my mouth to speak, but she continued. "Your own thoughts about this are what's creating the fear. Please remember that Ring doesn't live in your head, and that the Ring you imagine walking is not the Ring who's in the lodge right now with Robert. You're attached to your own thoughts and fears, and it's that attachment that is causing you to suffer in this way about him."

I was incredulous. "You don't eat meat," I said. "You believe in not hurting animals. You think it pollutes your mind and body to do that. So how can you say it's okay to make Ring walk the pillars?"

"We try to do no harm. But in some situations, harm will be done no matter what we do. We let you come here, and Viviana, and we'll let you walk the pillars if you decide that's what you need to do when you're ready, when you have clarity. Neither of you is dying. Many people would say we're harming you by giving you this option. You don't think so because you're suffering. To you, right now, unbearable suffering seems like the only alternative to walking. So there's harm either way. Even Robert, who knows if he could last longer, and with less physical discomfort, if he were in hospice care instead of here meditating and planning to walk thirteen miles in the snow. But doing this involves less fear for him, less suffering, and he only feels able to do it with Ring. And he feels sure that Ring going with him is what will cause the least suffering for Ring, too."

"It's not that I don't understand what you're saying. It just still seems like killing Ring, even though he might have a hard time if he were left without Robert. This doesn't seem like a philosophical matter to me. It just seems wrong."

Catherine nodded. "To be honest, that was my initial reaction too when I first spoke to Robert about it on the phone. But the more I talked to him, the more I understood the kind of judgment I was making. Robert pointed out that he couldn't come here without Ring, and that if he died in a hospital, Ring would be sent to a shelter, and the shelters where he lived were not no-kill. Ring's old for adoption, and even if he went to a no-kill shelter, he might stay there a long time or not get adopted at all. Robert doesn't want that to happen to him and doesn't want him to end up being euthanized without anyone who loves him being there with him."

Maybe Catherine could tell I was skeptical of this explanation, because she continued calmly but with an intonation like she was arguing a point rather than simply explaining something. "It's not an uncommon fear. When I was an oncology nurse, I had a few patients who wrote wills directing their animals to be euthanized after their deaths, because they were worried about what would happen to them otherwise."

"That doesn't make it okay, that other people have done it. Ring's a great dog. Someone would have taken him. Did Robert even try to find him a home?"

"Robert doesn't have any friends or family who would take him. He actually doesn't have much in the way of family or friends at all." Catherine looked down a little, and for the first time, it seemed to me that she wasn't entirely sure of what she was saying. "Robert explained that Ring's a very sensitive dog and gets depressed like a human does, and that sending him to a shelter felt like abuse. As Robert reminded me, all euthanasia of animals is a choice we make for them, trying to determine what's in their best interests. Everyone makes different decisions about this. Even veterinarians say that we need to be cognizant of the quality of an animal's life, not just the quantity. That when they have more bad days than good, it may be time to let them go."

"My parents kept saying that about my dog Daisy when she got old. I didn't agree with it then. They told me I'd understand when I grew up, but you know what? I really don't. What does 'quality of life' even mean? It's so ambiguous. It just seems like something people say to justify being selfish, to avoid the responsibility of taking care of an animal when things get hard, to make it seem like they'd be better off dead."

I realized, after saying this, that Robert didn't have the option of taking care of Ring when things got hard. "Or finding someone else to take care of them when it gets hard. And what does 'more bad days than good' even mean? That it's okay to take an animal's life if they're unhappy fifty-one percent of the time? We don't do that to humans. Why is it okay with a dog?" I was starting to choke up and could feel tears welling up behind my eyes. I felt like I was in Alice in Wonderland. "And no one even knows for sure how unhappy Ring would be."

"You make some good points." Catherine nodded very slowly while looking directly at me, then raised her eyebrows a little. "Something to think about," she said, not taking her eyes off me. "What does quality of life mean, and is it okay to take a life based on it being unhappy?"

GRATITUDE CANDLES

As we parted in the kitchen, Catherine asked me to join everyone in the lodge two hours later for Robert's gratitude candles ritual. Robert would have sixty-eight candles, one for each year he'd completed in this lifetime. He would remember what he was grateful for in each year, thank everyone he wanted to thank, and extinguish the relevant candle. The last candle would be kept burning through the night and in the meditation hut the next day, the flame transferred as the candle burned down, for Robert to extinguish as he left the hut Thursday morning for the first pillar.

When I entered the lodge, Robert and Ring were sitting together on one of the couches in front of a low table filled with white candles in candle holders. Viviana and Catherine were sitting on chairs facing Robert, and there was an empty chair on each side of them. I sat in the chair next to Viviana. Robert's face looked different than the night before, more noticeably yellow and thinner, and his eyes looked mildly sunken. Ring was on one side of him, sitting up on his haunches, and on the other side was a small pile of paper sheets ripped out of a spiral notebook. Everyone was silent, waiting for Samu, who appeared shortly wearing purple pile pants and what looked, inexplicably, like a skullcap. He took the seat next to Catherine, who began to speak.

"We're here to celebrate the sixty-eight years of Robert's life and to witness and magnify his gratitude for these years." With this, she struck a match and started lighting the candles one by one, starting with the candle at the far-left corner and proceeding along that row, then moving back to the beginning to start the second row. We all remained quiet, watching the growing number of flames. Ring started shifting and emitting a low whine, which prompted Robert to put his arm around him and hug him to his body.

"He's never liked open flames," Robert offered. "It's okay," he now said to Ring. "Last time, I promise."

When all the candles were lit, Catherine put her hands together in prayer position, touched them to her heart, bowed her head, and quietly said, "Robert, whenever you wish to begin, we're here and listening."

Robert took in a deep breath and picked up the papers from the couch. He then closed his eyes for a moment, stood up, and picked up the first candle that Catherine had lit.

"In the first year of my life, I am grateful for my birth and for the love and care of my parents. I thank my mother, who carried and bore me; my father, who provided the seed of my existence and supported my mother; and every doctor and nurse involved in my birth. I also thank my grandparents, and their parents, and all of my ancestors for the creation of new lives that led to my existence in this lifetime. I thank my mother, who stayed home with me and helped me learn to crawl, who nursed me for the first months of my life, nourishing me from her own body. I'm thankful to my older brother who, though a young child himself, was gentle to me and never harmed me, and to our dog Ribbons for watching over me in my crib." With that, Robert blew out the candle and placed it back in its holder.

He then picked up the second candle. "In the second year of my life, I'm grateful that I developed into a strong and healthy toddler and learned to walk. I'm thankful to my mother's mother, Rose, who took care of me and my brother during the day when my mother went back to work." He blew out the candle, returned it to its place at the table, and picked up the third candle.

Robert continued in this way, reliving his childhood, his teenage years, college and graduate school. At twenty-four, he was thankful for meeting his ex-wife and for the love they shared in the early years of their marriage, and later for the birth of his son. At the mention of his son's birth, Robert started crying, holding the candle for his twenty-eighth year slightly forward and away from his torso so that his tears would not extinguish it before he was ready.

He was thankful for his career in mechanical engineering, for a good boss who helped him excel, for a difficult boss who helped him learn to stand up for himself. For milestones in his son's life, for the people who sustained him during and after his divorce. He was grateful for projects he completed, volunteer work he did, pieces of music that moved him, for his sister, who lived with and took care of his mother during the last years of her life; for his brother's wife, who held his brother close and cared for him with love as he declined from colon cancer.

In his fifty-ninth year, Robert was grateful for Ring, who he adopted as a puppy from a public shelter, and who helped him with his anxiety and later with the stress of his illness, who was there for him during a period of his life when he felt alone and scared. Robert pressed Ring to his side while he spoke of the way he and Ring had grown together until they got to the point that neither wanted to be separated from each other for more than an hour at a time, how even leaving Ring in order to run errands had become difficult, how Ring insisted on going everywhere with him until he realized that couldn't leave him when he died, that they'd need to stay together until the end.

As Robert described this, I had trouble suppressing the feeling that he was exaggerating it for his own purposes. I thought of the time I'd spent with Ring. Admittedly, it had only been in small increments, but he'd seemed fine going outside with me and Viviana. He'd been excited and happy to see Robert when they reunited, but I wasn't sure he was as dependent on Robert as he made him out to be.

But looking at Robert, gaunt and yellow with tears streaming down his face, I felt some guilt at having these thoughts. Regardless of how much Ring needed Robert, Robert did seem to need Ring, and this was a ceremony marking the end of Robert's life, so I tried to put the thoughts aside and concentrate on listening to his memories.

In his sixty-seventh year, Robert was thankful that after more than a decade of estrangement, his son agreed to speak to him, and they were able to share love and appreciation and forgiveness. He didn't explain why they'd been estranged, and it sounded like, when they did speak, it was only the one time, so that Robert could tell him he was sick and planning to go to the sanctuary.

When there was only one lit candle left, Robert picked it up. With tears running down his face and his voice hoarse with emotion, he looked at all of us.

"I'm grateful for cancer, for what it's helped me learn. I'm grateful for silence, for knowing what I want and need to do, for the chance to end my life with clarity and dignity, closer to God, part of God. I'm grateful to my doctors who offered me expert care, and who didn't fight with me when I declined most of it. I'm grateful to my son for understanding that I didn't want to die in a hospital. I'm grateful for Catherine and Samu, who have taught me... everything. I'm grateful for this sanctuary, for the Society, for stillness, for heat, for cold. I'm thankful to Ning, who kept me company here until she left to walk. I'm grateful to Viviana and to Lee for their company these last days. I'm grateful for Ring, who has been my partner this past decade, and who will be my partner to the end. I'm grateful to God, of which I am a part, and to which I am returning."

With that, Catherine took the last candle from Robert, still lit, and put it back in its holder.

DAY FIVE

I had been dreaming of Rachel, but on waking, I immediately knew she was gone. I knew where I was, and I knew what day it was. I knew I needed to get dressed and start the day with heat and cold, followed by yoga and meditation. And then I would watch Ring. I felt resigned, as though the final straw had been pulled out in a game of jackstraws, and I had reached the point where everything was at ground level.

When I got to the sauna room, Viviana was already there. I went to the kitchen and used the time to make my blended drink.

Once I was in the sauna with the timer set, I focused on my breathing, on the air pushing my belly out and my exhale pulling it back in. When thoughts arrived, of Robert and Ring, I started counting my breaths, slowing them as much as I could. I could feel the sweat running down my shins, down the side of my remaining breast, dripping from my forehead into the corners of my closed eyes.

Once in the shower, I noticed how much longer I was able to stay in the cold stream after only a few days of practice. I felt breathless but I counted the seconds and when they reached thirty, my breathing eased. I began to feel physically invigorated. I turned the water to warm, aware that even slightly warm now felt comfortable, and washed my skin and hair, then turned it cold again and counted another thirty seconds. When I left the shower stall, the energy in my body felt palpable, intense, at such contrast with the calm resignation I felt mentally.

Once I was dressed, I retrieved my drink and made my way to the lodge. Viviana was lying on her back on the yoga mat, breathing deeply into her belly and raising her hands up and down. I unfurled a mat next to her and lay down. As we moved through our routine of sun salutations, balance poses, and warrior stances, neither of us spoke. I followed her lead, shifting my feet when she did, bending when she bent, putting my hands together by my heart between poses as she did.

I was surprised by the ease with which my body moved through the postures, with the energy left over from the heat and cold therapy. I had never done yoga so soon after coming out of the sauna and cold shower, nor had I ever stayed so long in the cold water. It was if a younger version of my body had stepped in for the morning, carrying me through the routine.

When we finished and lay in corpse pose, I felt the energy moving freely through my limbs and torso. It felt like a faint humming, like a joining with some mild and nourishing electric current. I did not think of anything. I was neither lost nor missing anyone or anything; I just was.

After the yoga, I had my drink in the main room with Viviana. Neither of us had spoken yet that morning. There was no need to speak, or any expectation of talking. We were both fully aware of where we were, what we were doing, and what we were about to do.

After putting on our outer layers, we made our way out onto the walkway in the dark bracing cold. I felt the air enter my lungs, but was no longer surprised by it. The slight sting felt good, alive.

We turned onto the snow path and made our way to the meditation hut.

So Ham: I Am That

In the center of the hut was the last burning white candle. Around it sat Robert, Samu, and Catherine on meditation cushions. Ring was in Robert's room, waiting for me.

Catherine waved her hand toward the remaining two cushions, and Viviana and I sat on them, completing a circle around the candle.

Catherine started chanting, in low, drawn-out tones: "Sooo Haaam, Sooo Haaam." We all joined her, and our voices together were resonant. My eyes were closed, and I felt the vibrations from my own voice cohere with the vibrations from the other voices, until it was as if we were all together inside some kind of vibrating sound machine, the sound inside and outside at the same time, surrounding us and filling us, connecting us, becoming us.

Eventually, Catherine's voice lowered, and the rest of us lowered our voices in response, the vibrating fullness of our sounds becoming softer and softer until we were practically whispering. And then there was silence.

I continued in my head, as I'd been instructed, focusing on the sounds "So Ham." I became nervous and started thinking about having Ring for the rest of the day. Catching myself, I redirected my thoughts, first to wishing Robert well on his journey and then back to "So Ham." Over and over I did this as soon as I realized that my mind had wandered to Rachel, to Susan, to the thought of Robert and Ring walking out into the snow. Each time I redirected my thoughts to wishing Robert well, and added wishes for Ring, and then returned to "So Ham."

Several times I became restless, wondering how long I'd been meditating, wondering how I would know when I'd done enough and it was time to leave and get Ring. Catherine had said I would know, but I didn't. My legs felt uncomfortable, but was that the sign I was looking for, the indication that I was ready? Then I realized that this wondering, too, was a distraction of thoughts, and returned to wishing Robert and Ring well and to the mantra "So Ham."

And then I knew, all at once, that I was done. The thoughts that entered my head were less like distractions and more like greetings back to the outside world. I opened my eyes and saw the other four sitting upright on their cushions, eyes closed, intent and yet relaxed. I studied Robert carefully, unsure if I'd see him again before he left the following morning, if I would be returning Ring to him tonight or if Catherine or Samu would be getting him for Robert. Robert's face looked gaunt, and as I watched, he sighed and slowly lay down on the floor of the hut, hands on his belly, and continued meditating.

I rose and left the hut.

COHERENCE

When I opened the door, I found Ring lying on Robert's bed. He seemed like he'd been expecting me, but couldn't muster the energy to do more than acknowledge I was there—he moved only his head, which he stretched backward to look at me with his dark eyes. I walked over to the bed, sat down next to him, and stroked his side with my hand.

"Hey, I'm your buddy for the day while Robert prepares for your journey." I immediately regretted raising this specter for myself. My chest contracted, and I felt tears rising behind my eyes. I thought I should stand up and get Ring to follow me out of the room, take him to the lodge or maybe on a walk outside, though I was worried about taking him near the courtyard while everyone was meditating. While I considered what to do, I found myself, almost without will, sliding down onto my back next to him on Robert's bed.

Ring was on his side, and I turned until my stomach was against his back, spooning him. He stretched his head back toward me again and licked my face. I closed my eyes and focused on the way his tongue felt wet and soft on my cheek. I felt him lick my eyes, a weird melding of his saliva and the dampness of my own tears welling up. When he stopped, I kissed the top of his head, and he turned his head forward again, away from me, then sighed and rolled onto his back with his belly in the air. He wanted a belly rub.

I tried to do as Catherine said. Breathing in the musty, almost sweet smell of his fur, I moved my awareness into my right hand as it dragged over his belly, feeling the wispier, thinner fur and the occasional small bump of a nipple. I felt the way his rib cage peaked like a hill, so different than the flatter ribs on my own chest. I felt his belly rise and fall with his breath, the way Samu had instructed me to breathe. It was so natural for Ring that he seemed to do it without trying. I moved my own breath into my belly, imitating him, and tried to match his rhythm. We stayed like that for a while, breathing into our bellies, my hand softly stroking the fur on his chest and stomach, me looking at him and him looking at the ceiling.

When Ring had enough belly rubs, he rolled onto his stomach, sighed loudly again, and pushed with his front legs until he was in a sitting position. He then shook himself all over and, suddenly perky, jumped off the bed, went to the door, and stood there expectantly. Clearly, it was time to go. I didn't feel like moving, but Ring looked so certain that the door was about to open that I couldn't bear disappointing him, so I too sighed and got off the bed.

"Where do you wanna go?" I asked him. As we stood there, me looking down at him and him looking up at the doorknob, I realized, with a sinking feeling, that I was waiting for him to answer. I rubbed my eyes and face with my hands. Then I put my hand on the door, sighed again, and opened it.

I decided to follow him.

Ring led me through the hallway to the kitchen, then sat down there in the middle of the floor, looking expectantly at me again.

"Uh uh. I was not told to feed you anything. You may have a different recollection of events, but Robert said you're not allowed to eat in here." Ring kept staring at me, with a look that registered both hope and something akin to feeling sorry for me, like he was sure that I would give him something and he felt bad about me being so gullible. "Uh uh," I repeated. "Let's go to the lodge."

He just sat there looking at me. And then I remembered why I was with him, and what he was doing the next day, and I felt a lump in my throat.

"What can you even eat in here, anyway?" I asked. "It's all vegetarian." His ears pricked up a little.

I had never seen Robert feed Ring. I assumed he did it in his room, with regular dog food, but I realized I had no idea. I started looking around. In the refrigerator was a container with cooked lentils. I looked at it and looked at Ring, who seemed a bit hopeful. I grabbed a small plate, put a spoonful on it, and lowered the plate to the ground. I was surprised to see him jump up, put his head down to the plate, and inhale the lentils so fast he looked like he was snorting them.

"Really?" I asked. "You like lentils?" I thought about it and remembered that at dinner a few days back, he'd eaten a small piece of my broccoli. "You want some broccoli, too?"

Ring looked pretty satisfied, like he had properly educated me in communication skills. He waited in place while I found him a stalk of broccoli. It was raw. He took it in his mouth and wagged his tail, then lay down and started gnawing on it like a bone. I sat in one of the chairs by the table and watched him. He was completely pleased. And completely present. It was just him and the broccoli stalk.

I meditated on Ring eating the broccoli stalk. I slowed my breathing and watched him enjoy it. Whenever a thought entered my head, or the ache in my chest grew stronger, I returned my attention to Ring's teeth on the stalk, to his tail sporadically wagging, to how complete he seemed.

Rachel was still there in the background of every thought and feeling, underneath it all and surrounding it all. But watching Ring eat the broccoli, I started to feel like I was inside some sort of bubble with him and that time had stopped—was irrelevant even. That everyone and everything I'd ever loved was sitting in that bubble with us, infusing me while I breathed and watched him chew.

When he finished, he got up and walked over to me. I took his face in my hands, bent down, and rested my forehead on his head. We stayed like that for a minute or two and then, finished with the moment, he licked my face and walked to the door.

At which point I realized, for the first time in a long time, that I was hungry. I made myself a green drink and then we walked to the lodge.

I headed straight for a couch to lie down on, but Ring went and sat by the wood stove, which was cold. He looked at me the way he had in the kitchen.

"I know you like the fire, but they only do that at night. It's barely even afternoon. Come over here." I patted the couch. Not taking his eyes off me, Ring slowly lowered himself into a prone position.

I thought about it. They were all meditating with Robert and would be for hours. Would they really care? Did it matter?

"It's been a long time since I've built a fire, buddy," I said. "You may be sorry you asked."

But once I had it going, I realized he was right; it felt good, calming, warm. It felt like everything I wanted to feel. He had moved away from the stove while the door was open and I was working on the fire, but as soon as I closed the door, he came back and laid down right in front of it. I sat there with him, staring at the flames, until it got warmer and he got up and moved about ten feet away. I moved back as well, and lay down on the floor next to him. I matched my breathing to his again, and matched the rhythm of my hand stroking his side to both our breathing. I could feel his heartbeat, and I could swear I felt it change, along with my own heartbeat, until there was coherence. And something quieted inside me.

I don't know how long we slept like that, but it must have been a long time. When I opened my eyes, the light was almost gone. It must have been after three o'clock. I felt a small sense of panic, not remembering why I was on the floor or if there was somewhere else I was supposed to be. As it all came back to me, I realized there was nothing, really, that I needed to do, other than continue keeping Ring company. I remembered why with a pang.

I put my arm over his side, and he turned and licked my face.

When Catherine came looking for us that evening, we were still in the lodge. I had taken Ring outside a couple of times to relieve himself, but each time we returned to the big room. It was the only place either of us wanted to be.

The fire was out, and we were lying on a couch in the corner. I was awake but Ring was snoring. Catherine gently woke him by petting him and saying his name, and told me it was time to take him out to Robert in the meditation hut, where they would both spend the night before starting their trek the next morning. Robert was fasting. Catherine said she'd take Ring to his room and feed him, then bring him and Robert's backpack out to Robert, and then return with Samu and Viviana to start on dinner. I nodded mutely.

I wanted to give Ring a kiss, but my limbs froze and I couldn't move. As Ring followed Catherine out of the lodge, he looked back at me once, his eyes dark and round.

RECKONING

I woke many times that night. While I slept, I had my usual restless dreams, but they weren't about Rachel. They were about Ring walking endlessly in the snow. I tried breathing exercises. I tapped. Instead of the heaviness I normally felt in bed, I felt agitated, and like I needed to keep moving my legs. I had no idea what time it was any of the times I awoke. The long dark periods of the subarctic days and nights made it difficult to place myself in time, giving the entire night a hallucinatory feel. Wakefulness bled into dreams, which bled into being awake again, with no sense of minutes or hours, just an awareness of my heart beating against my shirt.

Eventually, I got up to check the time, but my cell phone had run out of battery. I did not bother to charge it. I threw on my overclothes and walked to the kitchen, where I saw it was three a.m.

I remembered the motherwort and sage tea and made myself a cup. As I sat at the table sipping it, I wondered if I should try to sleep again or, if not, what I should do.

I finished the tea, washed the cup, and headed back to my room. I put on my parka, boots, gloves, and hat, and grabbed a foil blanket. I wanted to go to the platform and lie down and look at the stars, but as I made my way outside, I suddenly remembered that Ring and Robert were sleeping in the meditation hut. I paused in the courtyard, afraid I would wake them. When I heard nothing, I proceeded more slowly, carefully placing each foot so there was no crunching of the snow.

I lay down on the platform wrapped in the blanket, looking up. The stars were so clear. I could never see the stars like this back home. I supposed Rachel must have seen them in the desert, and I wondered if she ever lay on the ground watching them as I was doing now. I saw a group of stars that looked like her—a Rachel constellation. Her long hair, her sandals were all there in the stars.

"Are you there?" I whispered.

"Please tell me you're here."

"I don't know why I'm here without you. I'm planning to join you. I want to know what you think of that. I need to know what you think I should do, whether you ever imagined this happening when you went down there. If you thought about what we'd do without you. I haven't even spoken to your mother in months. When you left, it was like a crack started at the foundation and just kept cracking, splitting everything open and apart. And now here I am, as far from the desert as possible, and yet in the desert nonetheless. Please tell me you're here."

The silence was loud and palpable. It was like another being, there with me in the dark. No insect sounds, no animals. Such silence that I could hear my own heartbeat, and it sounded like footsteps walking toward me.

And then it happened. The green light came, quickly this time, as if it were shooting across the sky with narrow tendrils that looked like wisps radiating off of something I couldn't see. My breath caught, as I did not expect to see the light this close to morning. I didn't even know it was possible. But it came. And I knew it was her.

And then, just as quickly, it was gone.

DEPARTURE

About an hour later, I heard stirrings in the meditation hut. I didn't move. After a few minutes, the door of the hut opened and Robert emerged slowly and, it looked, somewhat painfully. He was wearing his parka and backpack and walking on snowshoes. Behind him, Ring trudged over the snow in his little red coat and boots. He wasn't running or playing this time, just walking behind Robert and looking at the back of his knees.

Neither seemed to know I was there. I felt a sudden and strong urge to jump up and run after them and beg Robert to leave Ring at the sanctuary. How could I just lie here, allowing him to be marched to his death, and not do something? I felt sure I needed to act, but also completely helpless.

I couldn't stop Rachel from going to the desert to volunteer. I couldn't convince her to come back. My fear when she started tracking border patrol maneuvers and documenting them online—I had largely just swallowed it, because I saw how much Susan's outpourings of anxiety irritated her. Would it have been different if Susan had been more restrained? Was my own reticence just a reaction, a counter-pressure, an attempt to balance her out? Or was that giving myself too much credit?

Maybe part of me appreciated how much closer Rachel felt to me when she was upset with Susan. Was it possible that, in casting myself as the protector of Rachel's freedom, I was really just protecting my position as the favored parent? Did a part of me feel that was more important than Rachel's own safety?

What if I'd gone in person and begged her to stop, made her get in the car and come home? What if Susan and I had both gone, dropped to our knees, cried like babies, had promised to sign our home and all our funds over to the organization she'd joined? There was surely something I could have done. She was young and healthy and she went and I didn't stop her and she died. I didn't protect her. The only thing I ever swore to do in my life, and I hadn't done it.

I could hear Robert and Ring walking farther away, the crunching "whoosh" sound as Robert's snowshoes hit the ground, fainter and fainter. Every few seconds, I started to sit up or opened my mouth to yell. But nothing moved, and no words came out. I saw myself running after them, shouting to Robert to stop, somehow convincing him that despite the months he'd spent planning this, he hadn't thought it through clearly, that Ring should stay at the sanctuary.

I had working limbs; I could try to hold Ring, try to lead him back. It wasn't that taking action was impossible. It was very clearly possible, and yet I lay there, frozen in stillness, listening to the soft distant crunching of the snowshoes and the deafening, interminable pounding of my heart.

THE ICEMAN

At breakfast, no one spoke much. We each made our green drinks and then Catherine talked about the schedule for the day. Viviana's remained the same as it had been prior to Robert's last meditation. But mine was changing. It was time for me to learn the techniques of the Iceman.

"Have you heard of Wim Hof?" Catherine asked. I had not.

"He's a Dutchman who figured out how to control his autonomic nervous system."

I looked at her blankly.

"It's actually nothing new. Buddhist monks have been doing it for centuries, but he's developed some techniques that make it easier to teach people who haven't been meditating for decades. He's learned how to breathe in a way that super-oxygenates his blood, which allows him to hold his breath for long periods of time, control his body temperature, fight illness. He also does cold therapy to prepare his body, and psychological practices to control his mind. The result is that he can spend long periods of time in the cold and ice without getting hypothermic. He can do things like climb mountains in shorts, and run marathons in the desert."

At the word "desert," my stomach clenched. I put down my drink, which I was having trouble swallowing.

"You've already been practicing a little of what he recommends, with the hot-cold practice in the sauna and shower, and you've been learning to control your breath. But at this point, we're going to teach you more intensive breathing exercises and cold therapy ... also start you on some snowshoeing and more advanced mindset exercises. So go to the greenhouse as usual, but after yoga, join Samu in the meditation hut to learn the first breathing practice."

The words "meditation hut" also made my stomach tighten.

I did as she said. I went to the greenhouse, where the board said to pick scallions, kale, and broccoli, to weed the onions, and to water the green beans. I started with the scallions, but quickly found myself lying on the dirt floor staring at the plastic on the ceiling.

"What am I doing here?" My mind spoke softly but firmly. "How does becoming an ice man help me die in the snow? Why do I need help to die if that's what I want to do? Why did I even come here?"

I stood and started to put my parka back on to go outside for a few minutes, then stopped and put it back on the hook. I walked out into the walkway in just my under layers. It was dark and bitterly cold. I stood there in the walkway, closed my eyes, and felt the cold on my skin, in my lungs, on my eyes. How long could I stay like this? Why not just stay forever, right here under this covered walkway, conscious as long as I could be, then unconscious, then gone? Why wait until I've mastered staying alive in the cold, only to go out in it to die? What sense did any of this make?

I sat down. I watched the smoke of my breath. How long would it take?

The skin on my hands started to hurt first, then my eyes and eyelids. I opened my mouth and breathed through my mouth. It stung my lungs. This was what I wanted. I lay down. Through my shirts, the cold of the walkway bit my back. I closed my eyes.

First I saw the lights behind my eyelids. Then Rachel's face, the wisps of overgrown curly brown hair hiding one eye. I wanted to reach out and brush it aside. But next I saw Catherine coming to find me dead or unconscious on the walkway, calling for Samu, figuring out what to do with me dying like this out of turn, with no ritual or announcement, just because I wanted to.

My skin hurt all over now. I could see the stars when I opened my eyes, but the air stung my eyeballs. It felt like someone was vacuuming the fluid off them, like they were cracking. I suddenly couldn't remember where I was, had to reach far into my mind through slow-moving thoughts that slipped my grasp as soon as I touched them. I wanted to go to sleep. Why shouldn't I go to sleep?

And then, for reasons I don't understand, I rolled over, pushed myself onto my knees, and crawled back to the greenhouse.

WAITING TO INHALE

"Lee, you'll see," Samu said. "This is so good. You think you don't have control over what happens in your mind, in your body. You can have control over it. You can walk thirteen miles in the snow in shorts and feel good. You'll see!"

"Why would I want to do that? I thought the whole point of walking was to…"

Samu stared at me, waiting for me to finish the sentence.

"You know…. I thought the cold is what helps, in the end, by freezing you. Why does it help to be able to control that?"

Samu blinked as if he didn't understand.

"Lee, you want to kill yourself?"

He looked so honestly puzzled that I didn't know what to say. Yes, I came here for help with that. It's what they advertised.

"If you want to kill yourself, you can leave here, go home, or go somewhere else and do that. You don't need to come here to do that."

He looked at me. I looked at him.

"You traveled a long way to come here. I think you came here to learn how to control your mind and body, to be conscious in whatever you're going to do. If all you want is to kill yourself, then what are you waiting for?"

"I don't know. Maybe I'm scared. Maybe I just want it to feel safe."

"You want it to feel safe to kill yourself?"

"Maybe I want to feel some sense of peace first."

"Well, this is your sense of peace first, Lee. The Iceman knows sense of peace. Did you know he can clear his blood of injected E. coli in fifteen minutes? He teaches how to do that. He taught me how to do that. That is peace."

"Why would you inject E. coli into your body?"

"To clear it. To clear the E. Coli."

Now I looked at him blankly.

"To control your immune system. Your nervous system. Peace is not up here." He tapped his head with his index finger. "Peace is in your body. You need to feel your body to feel peace. You … you don't feel your body most of the time. I think that's why you came here, at least part of it. You want to feel your body. You can't feel it."

He closed his eyes, took a deep breath, and looked at me again.

"You feel your body, you feel peace. You still want to die? OK! Then you know what you are doing, what you are leaving, and why. You don't throw yourself into a situation you hope you can't get out of and then just wait for it to happen. You touch God, you touch the seven pillars. This is the third and the seventh pillar, what the Iceman taught me. It is air and ice. You learn this, then you feel peace and know what you're doing, and then you make your choice. You want the cold to kill you? You invite it in, you don't just go so far away no one can help you and then let it chase you down like prey. You aren't prey, Lee. You are the hunter. You are hunting yourself."

"Samu, you're a vegan."

"It's a metaphor," he said. "You know what a metaphor is?"

So much for my attempt at a joke. Embarrassed, I nodded.

"There's a difference between lying on the ground helpless and waiting to die—yes, I saw you earlier—and being part of the universe, present, in control of your own mind and body, and deciding what you need to do. You are not a victim, you know? You have experienced really tremendously difficult things, but the idea isn't to curl up and wait to be hit more. It's to get yourself back, to tap into the energy of life, to feel the peace of the body, and *then* decide what you want to do. Clearly. Peacefully."

I nodded again. And looked at the ground.

"Lee, why did you come here, eh?"

I was silent for a while.

"The snow, I guess. The structure of the thing. Having people to leave. There was no one left to leave. I guess I didn't want to go through it alone, wanted to be able to say goodbye to someone and have them know what I'm doing, and not be surprised to find me. To have everything taken care of afterwards." I thought about it, and in my mind, I just kept seeing vast expanses of snow, an image that had been comforting me for months, though I still wasn't exactly sure why. "Mostly, I guess, the snow."

"Okay, so the snow is what we're going to focus on a lot the next few days. Cold and breath. Snow. Ready? This first breathing exercise … it's so good."

Samu proceeded to teach me how to suck in oxygen forcefully and deeply through my nose and exhale quickly through my mouth. Sitting on the floor in case I got dizzy. Forty times in a row, then exhale all the way out and lie down and close my eyes. Don't inhale until I need to.

It was the calmest I had felt since being here, since losing Rachel, since possibly ever. Inside me, everything went dark and silent and still. There were no thoughts, just stillness, a stillness I was part of somehow, that wasn't separate from me but wasn't limited to me either. I was lost in the cool, still darkness until I felt something shaking my foot gently.

"Okay, Lee, that is excellent. Maybe inhale now. It's your first time."

I realized only then that I hadn't taken a breath, had not needed to. I had a pang of fear that perhaps I couldn't inhale any longer, that I wouldn't be able to when I tried. But I did it. I opened my eyes.

"How long was it?"

"Almost two minutes. Too long maybe for first time. But so good."

"Samu, I felt peace. I actually felt peace."

"Yeah, it does that. You oxygenated your blood. You only need to breathe for oxygen. If you oxygenate your blood, you can go without breathing for a bit, and it calms the nervous system."

"What about the cold?"

"You've started that already with the hot-cold. Soon you start ice baths."

"Ice baths?"

"Yes, Lee, you will love it. It's…"

"So good?" I asked.

"So good," Samu said, smiling broadly as if I had just paid him the highest compliment.

I stood to leave.

"Lee."

"Yes?"

"Wim Hof's wife killed herself."

"What?"

"The Iceman. He lost his wife to suicide. Had four children to take care of. That's when he developed these practices."

I was silent.

"You understand?"

RING

That afternoon I was supposed to meet Catherine in the meditation hut for a longer meditation session, and to learn more breathing exercises. Indian breathing exercises this time, called *pranayama*.

When I stepped onto the walkway, I moved the scarf down from my mouth and inhaled deeply and sharply. The air hurt my lungs, but it felt like something I needed. I closed my eyes and sucked the air in again. It was almost three o'clock, and the sun was starting to set. Behind my eyelids, I could see the burnished orange light of the sky. I realized I was breathing through my mouth, closed it, and inhaled through my nose instead. It was less sharp, but it stung the inside of my nostrils.

I opened my eyes. In front of me, beyond the meditation hut and coming toward it, was a small red shape. I squinted, unable to tell what it was. I didn't have my glasses, hadn't needed to wear them for anything. I leaned forward and squinted again, and the red shape got slightly larger and took on a darker, blackish tint at the front. It looked like…

I walked quickly, then jogged, out toward the platform that was between me and the red and black shape, picking up speed as I went until I was running as best I could in my boots and in the snow. It was Ring. He was running now too, and toward me.

"Ring!" I shouted. "Ring!"

I started crying. I held onto the hood of my parka, and I ran, pumping one arm and using the other to keep my hood in place.

At my shouts, Catherine opened the door of the meditation hut and looked at me, mouth open, then turned to look where I was looking. And just stood, silently, as Ring ran toward us.

Ring stopped running when he was a few feet in front of me. He stood there looking at me, with the strangest expression on his face. "What happened to you?" I asked. "Where's Robert?"

Catherine came out and stood with me, and I bent down and pressed

Ring to my side. But he backed out of my embrace, kept backing up, and then turned and ran a few feet back in the direction he came from.

"What's going on?" I asked Catherine.

"I don't know," she said. "Something's not right."

"Did Robert send him back?"

"I don't know. That wasn't the plan. I don't know."

We looked at each other.

"Keep him here, Lee. I'll get Samu."

A few minutes later, a wide-eyed Viviana came out the kitchen door, jogged over, and stood silently next to us. Then I heard the sound of the snowmobile. Samu was driving it. Catherine was sitting in the sled. As they went past us, Ring tried to turn and run after them, but Viviana said, "Lee, grab him! Let's get him inside. He can't keep up with the snowmobile and he already looks exhausted."

I grabbed onto the trim at the opening of Ring's coat and, with my other hand on his neck, guided him onto the walkway and back into the kitchen. Viviana stopped there, and I could see her shaking a little as she leaned back on the counter and covered her face with her hands. I continued with Ring out into the hall and into the lodge. "I'll start the fire," I told him. He just stood there looking at me, then sighed and climbed onto the nearest couch.

The Second Pillar

When I opened my eyes, the lodge was dark except for the low glow of the dying fire. I was lying on the couch wrapped around Ring, who was lying on his side and breathing deeply. Looking at him more closely, I saw that his eyes were open.

I gradually became aware of Catherine sitting on the chair next to the couch. I sat up, rubbing my eyes, and looked over at her, a pit in my stomach.

She was looking at the fire.

The last thing I remembered was burying my face in Ring's fur, relieved to feel his body against mine, and then the feeling that I was slowly sinking into some kind of dark and hazy space.

"What time is it?" I asked, disoriented.

"Five o'clock."

"In the afternoon or morning?"

"Afternoon."

We sat in silence. Ring lay still.

"Robert?" I asked.

Catherine looked at me and smiled weakly. "He was lying face down in the snow a little before the second pillar."

"Is he okay?"

"No, he's dead."

Silence.

"I don't understand."

"He must have had a heart attack or a stroke. He may have waited too long. His body just wasn't capable of making the full journey."

More silence.

"After all that, he didn't make it to the seventh pillar?"

Catherine smiled kindly. She turned to face me. "No."

I felt my heart beating against my clothes. It was so uncomfortable that I pulled at my shirt with my fingers, trying to move it farther away. This wasn't what walking was supposed to be like. It wasn't what death here was supposed to be like. Robert had worked so hard to die peacefully; it now seemed like that had been too much to ask. And Ring? What good did it do him to go through that? All the planning Robert had done, all of my arguing, and in the end none of it mattered. I put my hands over my eyes.

"It's okay, Lee. Robert's main journey was the last few months. He did what he needed to do."

"Where's his body?"

"We left it for now. We try not to touch the body for three days. This allows whatever's left of the spirit to orient itself and leave on its own."

The flame got lower. Catherine got up and fed the fire.

"What will you do in three days?"

"Robert wanted to be cremated and his remains sent to his son. Samu will bring his body to the funeral home in Attawapiskat in three days."

"Ring?"

Catherine sighed. "Ring."

We both watched the fire, and I ran my fingers through the black and white fur on Ring's side.

"We'll need to bring Ring to Attawapiskat too," said Catherine, shrugging her shoulders a little.

"Where?"

"I don't know. There's a vet who flies there from Winnipeg sometimes to treat and neuter the street dogs. A friend of Samu's works with her and sends dogs to her rescue, and he cares for them while they're waiting for the transport. Maybe they'll take Ring. I don't know yet."

"Can't he stay here?"

"For now, yes, but not permanently. Some of his food is left. He should eat. We haven't cleaned Robert's room yet, so it's still in there. Until Samu takes him to Attawapiskat, can you take over feeding and caring for him? Can you let him sleep in your room, or stay in Robert's with him?"

"Sure." I rubbed my eyes. My heart was still beating against my clothes uncomfortably. Suddenly, without warning, my chest and face shuddered and I sobbed, tears streaming from my eyes. I covered my face, tried to stop.

"Let it out," Catherine said. "You need to let it out."

I bent over Ring and held him close to me. He barely moved. Then he turned and licked my face.

ROBERT'S ROOM

Robert's room was bare except for a neat pile on the rocking chair consisting of two shirts, one pair of pants, two books, a case of canned vegan dog food, and a mostly empty large bag of vegan dry food. I looked around for a bowl but found none, so I went to the kitchen, Ring padding after me, and brought back an empty bowl and one half-filled with water. I put them both on the ground.

I was giving Ring a running monologue, explaining every step I was taking to try to get him fed. He politely tolerated my talking but his face gave the impression he found it uninteresting. When I stopped, he walked to the water and drank until he drained the bowl. I opened a can of the wet food and put it in the other bowl. Ring looked at it, looked at me, went over to the bed, jumped on it, and lay down.

"Sorry about the food, Ring, but I guess you've been eating like this since you got here. Catherine said they wouldn't let Robert bring any meat, that he had to order this and get it delivered to Attawapiskat for you. I didn't know there was such a thing as vegan dog food."

I shoved my hand into the bag of dry food until I reached the rough hard pieces near the bottom, and pulled out a few. I held them on my flat palm in front of his face. He sighed but did not move.

"You need to eat something."

No movement.

"Ring, you need to eat something." I sat down next to him and started petting his head softly. I put a piece of kibble between his lower lip and gum, hoping he would chew it. He didn't. He just lay there with it stuck between his lip and gum.

"I know what that feels like," I said. "Come to dinner with me. Maybe some broccoli will go down better." I got up and went to the door, but he didn't move. "Ring!" I called, and patted my thigh with my hand. He still did not get up.

"I'm not really hungry either," I said, and got into bed next to him. I lay on my side with my stomach against his back and put my arm over him. He sighed again.

"I'm so sorry. I'm really sorry. I'm so, so sorry," I told him over and over, feeling tears welling up behind my eyes but not coming out. A knot in my throat made it difficult to swallow. I could feel his breath so clearly against my stomach and the space where my breast used to be. The way he breathed with his whole body. I trained my breath to his, inhaled with my stomach and then my chest, the way he did, until we were breathing in synchrony. I could still feel my heart beating against his back, my chin buried in his fur.

Neither of us moved all night.

VIVIANA

Viviana was in the kitchen when I walked in, Ring behind me, to make my drink. Earlier, while lying in bed, I'd gotten Ring to eat a few pieces of dry food out of my hand but that was it. He did follow me to the kitchen, though, where I hoped to find something more tempting for him. I stopped when I saw Viviana.

"Hey," she said, not looking at me. I remembered her leaning against the counter yesterday, shaking, and realized I hadn't seen her since.

"Are you okay?" I asked her.

She put down the cucumber she was cutting in half, dried her hands on her pants, and turned to face me. "What does that possibly mean?" she asked.

"You're right. I'm sorry," I said, and opened the refrigerator to look for leftovers.

"It's okay," she said, and went back to making her drink.

Looking at her, it occurred to me out of nowhere that her hair was not growing, even though she'd been here longer than I had. It was still shorn close to her head. She must be trimming it, I thought, and then stood amazed at myself for thinking about something so trivial in the midst of the heaviness weighing down on the three of us. My own hair was pasted to my head and neck, and I disliked the feeling of it against my skin, having worn it short all my life.

"Do you think you could cut my hair?" I asked.

"What?" Viviana looked at me, bewildered.

"I'm sorry. I don't know why I care, but it's never been this long and feeling it against my neck is… I don't know… somehow making things worse. I thought maybe you'd have a trimmer with you. I'm sorry to ask right now. I don't know what I'm thinking, if I'm thinking…"

"I do, I brought one. I can do it if you want. I can't stand that feeling either. That's why I brought it with me. Catherine isn't thrilled about me using electricity for it, but it's quick with me. It'll take longer with you, and I think we may need to start with scissors."

I stood, feeling a little confused even though I was the one who had asked. It was as though we were standing in an envelope of still air, in the middle of something very heavy and weighted, and there was nothing happening— nothing to do or say, other than this incomprehensible conversation about hair.

Viviana spoke first. "Why don't we do it in the shower room? You'll want to wash the hair off after, so you may as well do your hot-cold therapy. Is that on your schedule for this morning?"

I nodded.

"Okay then, make your drink and meet me there. We can use the chair. I'll get the trimmer and ask Catherine for some scissors."

"Do you think she'll mind my wanting to do this?"

"I don't think so. Honestly, I think it's kind of a good sign."

I felt rankled by this statement. "I just don't like the way it feels against my neck."

Viviana smiled at me wanly. "At least you're aware of how your neck feels."

Later, as I sat on the plastic chair in the shower room with no mirror, I felt Viviana's fingers against my neck and occasionally the cold steel of the scissor blades. I heard repetitive small snips, jarring in the way they cut through the otherwise silent air, and was aware of small clumps of hair falling onto me and onto the floor. I closed my eyes. As Viviana's hand touched my neck, I realized it was the first skin-to-skin physical contact I'd had with another human in… months—I didn't know how many. As the snipping changed to the dull loud buzz of the trimmer, I kept my eyes closed, breathing into my stomach, feeling the hair, my hair, falling away into space.

THE ICE ROAD

My cold showers were now two-minutes long. Twenty minutes in the sauna and then two minutes under ice cold water in the shower as I focused on my breath and counting. Every morning, the first thirty seconds took my breath away and I felt as though I would die from lack of oxygen. But like clockwork, by thirty-five seconds, my breath returned to my control and the water felt warmer, though it was not. After two minutes, I turned the shower to warm, though I felt less and less like I needed to.

Samu was right. In the cold, the mind stops and all you feel is your body surviving. You are present. I was present. The ruminations ceased and everything was pared down to the cold and the breath and the body hanging on between the two. The Iceman discovered this as a way to survive his wife's suicide, to feel that she was gone but he was still here—just him and the cold—and it kept him going long enough to raise his kids. He became convinced that the brain is supposed to be in our control, that we can regulate mood and emotions and even our vascular system. Consciously regulate it— depression, anxiety, suicidality, resignation. Breath and ice. Breath and ice. Breath and ice. Until the body starts humming.

Ring had taken to waiting for me in the shower room. As I sat in the sauna box with my head sticking out, I talked to him in a running monologue.

Reviewed how much he'd eaten, how much I'd eaten, how he'd acted when we went outside in the snow for him to relieve himself. How each of the last two mornings he'd looked out toward the trail to the pillars but stayed with me, and how I hadn't had to ask him to. How he spent most of his time lying on his side and sighing. How he kept me warm at night, how my nervous system slowed and calmed with his back against my chest and his heart beat against my arm draped over his side.

While I reviewed all of this from the sauna, he would sometimes lift his head and one ear and look at me in contemplation, then drop his head back to the floor and sigh. After so many months of silence, I couldn't keep quiet when we were alone together. I told him about Rachel, how Rachel was my Robert, perhaps more so since I'd held her as a baby. Rachel was supposed to outlive me, but then Robert should have outlived Ring. I listened to Ring's breathing heavy against the floor and contemplated our shared situation, how we would get through the next hour.

As I left the sauna for the shower, Ring followed me with his eyes but continued to lie on his side on the wood floor. As I breathed and counted in the freezing water, I periodically called to him that I was okay, that I was learning to tolerate the cold. When I got out of the shower, I sat with him on the floor until it was time to go to the greenhouse. It went on like this for two days. On the second day, as we walked out the kitchen door to the walkway, we saw Samu riding off toward the pillars on the snowmobile with the sled behind it. I pulled Ring to my legs and led him into the greenhouse.

When we emerged back into the kitchen carrying sheaves of kale and a small bucket of green beans, Catherine was there washing vegetables for a stew.

"Did they get back?" I asked.

"Yes."

"Where's his body?" I wasn't sure why I asked, as I didn't really want to know.

"It's still on the sled. Covered. Samu will take it to Attawapiskat soon. He'll take Ring as well."

"What?" I asked, feeling a cold tightness in my chest and aware of my pulse in my throat.

"He can't stay here indefinitely."

"You can't make him ride with Robert's body."

"It's covered. It's frozen. He's a dog."

Catherine looked at me.

"Animals don't have the same fear of death and bodies, Lee. It may make him sad, but he knows what happened. I don't think he's afraid and you don't need to be either. This happens to all of us. This will happen to you."

"I just can't imagine him riding…" I was at a loss, thinking of Samu driving off with Ring and Robert's body, taking Ring somewhere and leaving him there. "Do you know where he's going?"

"Each time the rescue comes, they take a bunch of dogs back to Winnipeg to adopt out. Samu's friend Matt takes care of some of the strays and keeps a list of which ones are ready for adoption and which ones need medical care. Samu's going to ask him if he can hold onto Ring until the next transport and get him on it. If he can't, he can at least help Samu figure out what to do. If anyone knows how to find a dog a home, it's Matt."

All I wanted to do was lie down on the kitchen floor, but instead I found myself asking, "Would it be okay if I go with them? To say goodbye to Ring, and see where he's going?"

An hour later, I was riding behind Samu on the snowmobile, with Ring fastened in the sled next to Robert's frozen body, which was inside some kind of red covering that looked like a giant duffle bag. Ring lay pressed against it, looking out behind the sled as it moved along.

The ride over the snow was long—longer than I remembered. The last time, it had been getting dark as we traversed this area, and all I remembered seeing was Samu's back and the stars coming out above us. Now the sun was out and the snow glittered, so much that sometimes my eyes hurt and I had to close them or focus on Samu's back.

But when I was able to look, I could see tufts of dried grass sticking up through the snow in places that had been windswept. I also saw stunted spruce and fir trees sporadically dotting the distance in two directions. Mostly, though, it was flat open space covered in shimmering snow. At one point, Samu pointed off to the left, and when I followed his finger, I could see something large and brown moving in the distance between two trees. Without my glasses on, it took me a minute to realize it was a moose.

When we got to the ice road, Samu fastened the sled to the motorcycle and I got in the side car. In the sun, the road's surface looked like it was encrusted with tiny diamonds. Even with the cold wind hitting the small pieces of skin exposed on my face, the glittering reminded me of the sand at White Sands. In fact, it seemed there was no difference, that at either end the extremes were the same, connected as in a circle. I could feel Rachel in my lap, seven years old, looking at the sand. The way she said she just wanted to stay there, watching handfuls of sand crystals slip silently through her fingers.

ATTAWAPISKAT

Once back in Attawapiskat, I was surprised by how small it seemed. My memory of the town was in still images: the river from the sky, the flap covering the window at the airport, Samu's curly hair when he removed his helmet. I couldn't place anything else.

We drove down a few snow-covered roads lined with trailers and small single-story houses, all with stove pipes sticking out of the roofs or walls. Some of the houses were in disrepair, with boards or tarps covering windows or roofs. Others had structures outside them that looked like tipis, a few with smoke coming out of the tops. I pointed to one and asked Samu whether people lived in them. He laughed.

"No. Those are smoke houses."

The roads didn't seem to be paved, but alternated between dirt and gravel as we wove through town. After a few turns, I realized that there were no signs anywhere, not even road signs. We drove by houses and a white clapboard church. Eventually, we passed a larger building with writing on its side indicating it was a grocery store with a Kentucky Fried Chicken inside. This was the first indication anywhere in town that someone might be driving through who didn't already know where everything was.

There were dogs on every street, walking or trotting between buildings, sitting in the snow. At one point, I gripped Samu as two dogs appeared to run at the motorcycle, but Samu hardly seemed to notice. I braced for impact and gasped, but he drove right past them and, as I looked behind us, I saw that the dogs didn't seem to notice anything amiss either, continuing to mill around in the road. I wondered what Ring was thinking, watching them run free like that.

"Whose dogs are those?" I asked Samu, then repeated the question more loudly so he could hear me over the noise of the motorcycle.

"They live here," he answered, shrugging his shoulders. I waited for the rest of his response, but that seemed to be the entirety of it.

Every couple of streets, we passed groups of teenagers ambling slowly, some laughing loudly or walking backwards for a few steps at a time in order to face the others. A few of them wore no hoods or hats but seemed unbothered by the cold.

We went to the only funeral home which, I was soon told, was the satellite office for a larger operation in Thunder Bay and associated with the cemeteries at the two Catholic churches here. It was the size of a small house, but built in a contemporary style that was out of place. Too much stained wood and too many windows for the climate. It looked recently constructed.

I sat with Ring in the sled while Samu went inside, completed some paperwork, and then allowed Robert's body to be lifted onto a long cart and moved into the building. I looked away while they moved his body, but the sound of it making contact with the cart made my stomach clench. I focused on my breathing and keeping an eye on Ring while Samu got the bike ready and I stepped back into the side car.

Samu next pulled up to a newish-looking green trailer. I could see the shadow of letters that been scraped off the front of the building. They spelled

"De Beers." I knew I had seen that word before but couldn't remember where. Above the front door was a small sign that said Youth Center Office.

Samu motioned to me to get out and went to unfasten Ring, removing a courier-style bag from the sled and putting it over his shoulder.

"Samu, if there's no vet here, what do people do if their dog gets sick?" I asked.

Samu shrugged. "People don't exactly keep dogs here the way you're used to. Some of the dogs are cared for by specific people, but a lot of them live on the street and take care of themselves. Matt looks out for some of them, but if they need vet care, they have to wait until the vets are flown in or Matt gets them on a transport."

I was startled by this information. I had purposefully come out here with no thought of medical care for myself, and was happy to do without it, but the thought of a sick dog having nowhere to go felt intolerable. I glanced at Ring.

I guess Samu saw the consternation on my face, since he stopped what he was doing and looked at me more carefully. "Lee, wild animals get sick too and most of them never see a vet."

I thought about that, and couldn't explain why it seemed different.

Once Samu finished unfastening Ring, I grabbed the edge of his coat and pulled him toward me out of the sled. He followed us to the trailer, looking down at the snow as he walked.

Samu climbed the two steps to the front door and knocked while Ring and I waited at the bottom. The door opened and a man with dark hair pulled back into a short ponytail looked at Samu with a slightly confused expression and then smiled.

"Samu! What the hell you doin' here?" he said.

"Hello, Matt!" Samu said with his usual cheer. "We had an unexpected event at the sanctuary and had to come into town, so I thought I'd come see you. I need your help with something." He turned and pointed at me and Ring. "This is Lee, a guest at the sanctuary, and that's Ring."

Matt, who appeared to be in his early forties and was wearing a checkered flannel shirt and jeans, looked from Samu to me and Ring and then back to Samu. "Bring me any vegetables?" he asked with raised eyebrows and a slightly mischievous grin.

"Always," said Samu, patting the bag on his shoulder.

"Well then, I guess I better invite you in before they freeze, eh." He smiled more naturally now, waving us all inside the trailer.

It was warm enough inside to remove my parka, but still chilly. Matt led us to a small table against the wall with several chairs in front of it, next to an open kitchen. He motioned for us to sit down and offered us tea, which we both accepted.

Neither Samu nor Matt seemed in any hurry to get to the reason for our unexpected visit. They appeared genuinely glad to see each other, and made small talk.

"Did you hear we had a polar bear wander into town last week?" Matt asked.

"What?" Samu looked surprised.

"I know. Something about the way the warming's changing the currents made the ice flow in the wrong direction, and he just walked right into town. It happened in Moosonee a few weeks ago, so we'd been warned. But we're not used to it and everyone's still on high alert." Matt looked at me and raised his eyebrows. "They can kill you."

Given his apparent eagerness to avoid the bears, I decided not to mention that I'd gone to Churchill because my daughter had wanted to see them.

Matt asked where I was from and nodded as I answered, filling a kettle with bottled water. "Can't use the tap water," he said in explanation. "Water's poisoned." I vaguely remembered hearing about this on the news at the hotel in Churchill.

Samu was watching Matt while taking the vegetables out of his bag one by one and putting them on the table. "How are your sister and her kids? I haven't seen them in ages."

"Good! They're at the hockey rink," Matt answered, turning on the stove.

"There's a hockey rink here?" I asked, surprised. The town seemed way too small to have its own rink. Then again, I couldn't think of how anyone would get to a rink in a bigger town.

"Yep," Matt answered. "You're in Canada." He turned toward me with a slight smile. "Well, you're not exactly in Canada. You're in a sovereign Nehiyawak—Cree—nation. But the obsession with hockey's the same." He took three mugs out of a cabinet and put a tea bag in each. "You play hockey?"

I shook my head and, glancing at me, Matt suddenly stopped smiling and looked like he felt bad for asking. I wondered how much he knew about the sanctuary, and what made his demeanor change like that.

But he recovered quickly. "There's not always a lot for the kids to do here, especially in winter. The rink's important to them. Not that that matters to everyone." He looked at Samu and shrugged, then added, "Anyways."

I squinted at him, trying to figure out what that could possibly mean.

"Sorry, it's a sore point when outsiders ask about the rink." Matt scowled briefly as the kettle started to whistle and he moved to turn it off.

I looked at Samu, confused.

Samu sighed and explained that a few years back, the community's ice resurfacer broke down and needed to be replaced. So the parents, grandparents, aunts, and uncles raised money to buy a new one and have it shipped up by barge. "It was a big deal. Months of bingo games, fundraisers, pooling money. You know, the kind of thing families in a community do to buy things for their kids. It had been hard for the teenagers here for a while. . ." Samu glanced at Matt. ". . . and hockey is such a positive thing for kids, so good. I remember feeling so happy when Matt told me the Zamboni finally arrived. Everyone was excited…" Samu trailed off and looked down at the table.

I was stuck on Samu saying that things had been hard for the teenagers. I remembered the reporter on the TV in Churchill talking about the attempted suicides and opened my mouth to ask about it, but didn't know how to broach the subject without sounding intrusive. Thoughts of Rachel passed through my mind, alternating between a fantasy of her sitting in the trailer with us and an image of her walking away from her car in the Arizona desert. I rubbed my eyes, trying to pay attention to the conversation.

Matt was quiet for a moment and looked at me like he was going to ask me something, but instead he picked up Samu's thread. "Then this columnist at the *Toronto Sun* wrote an opinion piece that was reprinted everywhere, saying that us buying the Zamboni proved Attawapiskat didn't really need more housing or money for health care or water treatment, because the families spent money on the Zamboni when they could have spent it on those things instead. That it meant the Chief and Council were mismanaging government accounts. Anyways."

I wasn't following. Which was fine, since I hadn't cared much about following conversations for a long time and this one didn't concern me or require a response. And yet once upon a time, I had worked on funding issues for a living, so my inability to understand what Matt was talking about bothered me in some small way I couldn't entirely shake. "I thought Samu said the parents raised the money for the ice refinisher," I heard myself say, my eyes squinting. "What does that have to do with the government?"

Samu smiled encouragingly and turned toward the kitchen. "Matt, Lee's a grant writer and knows a thing or two about funding."

Matt brought the tea over, handing each of us a mug, and sat down. The warmth of the mug in my hands seemed to clear my mind a little as he answered. "Yeah? Interesting. But I actually didn't mean to offer you a seminar on Attawapiskat's finances to go with your tea." I responded with something between a head shake and a shrug, hoping that was enough to indicate I didn't think he had, and he continued. "But yeah, I wanted to ask that guy, if parents in Toronto pooled money for hockey equipment or something else for their kids, did he think the provincial government should keep track of that and deduct it from public spending on health care or water treatment? The guy's a big conservative. Last I heard, they didn't think people's private property should be treated as belonging to the government. Except here, apparently... But also, you have any idea what building infrastructure or houses costs up here? A little more than a Zamboni." Matt blew on his tea.

I nodded and mumbled agreement that the criticism was stupid. I wondered when Samu was going to ask about Ring. But that didn't seem to be where Samu was heading.

"Matt," said Samu, even more animated than usual, "since Lee's a grant writer, maybe they have some ideas for you." I noticed that as Samu used my pronoun, Matt looked up at me for a second and smiled before looking back down to blow more on the hot liquid. I was surprised to feel a small amount of comfort from this. But then, realizing that Samu had also just offered my professional services, the feeling turned to low-level anxiety. Samu pressed on. "Lee, Matt runs the new youth center here. He's so good with the kids and he's always trying to figure out how to fund projects. Maybe the two of you can talk about some ideas."

This felt like it came out of nowhere, and I wasn't sure what Samu was trying to do. It was true that I'd been a grant writer for a legal aid organization back in Wisconsin, but that seemed like a lifetime ago and I didn't know anything about funding sources for youth programs in Canada. I felt my mouth drop open.

Luckily, Matt came to the rescue. "That's okay," he said. "I don't need that kind of help. I'm a pretty good grant writer. Normally I don't brag, eh. But there's no one here to brag for me right now." He winked again and I tried to smile a little. "In fact," he continued, "I just worked with an environmental organization to get iPads for a bunch of teenagers so they can make their own movies about living here. I have a certificate in public management from University of Toronto. Grant writing was part of it."

"Hey, I didn't know that," said Samu. "I'll brag for you. Lee, Matt's made such a big difference for the kids. He does so much. He also works with Shannen's Dream. Have you heard of it?"

I shook my head, relieved the conversation had moved on. "I'm embarrassed to say that almost everything I know about this area comes from my guidebook."

"Your guidebook?" Matt looked amused. "People still use guidebooks?"

"I guess I'm old," I offered.

Matt laughed. "Well, I guess I'm not surprised Shannen's Dream isn't in a guidebook. The only things Canadian writers seem to find interesting about this place are poverty and crisis, with a little traditional dancing and drumming on the side. Not exactly interested in our local initiatives. I'm sure your guidebook said we're poor, right?"

I nodded and looked back down at the table. "It had a lot of statistics." In fact, I realized, the part about Attawapiskat was mostly statistics.

Matt sighed. "Attawapiskat gets written about a lot. But mostly just things that make it seem hard to live here. Which then makes some people say we shouldn't live here at all. I don't see much written about the reasons we *want* to live here—our community, our land, what we do for ourselves and our kids. Just the housing in disrepair. And the unemployment and poisoned water. Like if you have something serious you're dealing with, that's it. That's all you're about. Poor Attawapiskat. Not poor enough to do anything about the underfunding and broken treaties, of course. Just poor enough to satisfy ideas about what a First Nation's supposed to look like. That's all most Canadians are interested in." He breathed out forcefully through his nose, in what sounded like a cross between a laugh and an exasperated sigh. "Though I hope a guidebook would say something nice about the place, if it's trying to get you to visit."

I contemplated this for a moment. It had to have said something else, but I couldn't remember anything specific. I'd only come the first time because it was the closest airport to the sanctuary, and now because I was worried about Ring.

"I don't remember what else it said," I offered a little sheepishly. "I think it had some information about the ice road, and maybe an inn. . ."

Matt nodded. "Kataquapit Inn, probably. . . Nothing about the landscape? This area's gotta be the most beautiful place on Earth—the river and the bay, the colors in the spring. But for some reason, that doesn't seem to interest people much." I remembered the silver snake of the river through the window of the plane as we landed, and the trees and vast expanses of snow as we approached the town today. He was right; I'd read nothing that came even close to describing what that looked like.

"I'd offer to show you around town, but I have a meeting in less than an hour. And Samu almost never stays that long." He raised his eyebrows at Samu.

"Hey!" Samu said, "You know I always have errands when I come in. And it's a long ride back to the sanctuary."

Matt laughed. "Well, since I can't show you around, maybe I should write a guidebook! You know, for when the market picks back up for guidebooks. . ." He winked, then sighed. "The written descriptions of this place just drive me a little crazy sometimes, and it pains me to think anyone would rely on them. It's like we can only be one thing. We're either completely traumatized and destitute, or we don't need anything at all. We can't be happy to live here and also need equitable funding and infrastructure. Every once in a while, when the Chief declares an emergency, some reporters fly in and ask a few questions. We get sound bites on TV about how dire the crisis du jour is, with the reporters looking very grave and very sorry, and then they leave. That's about it. Anyways." He shrugged again. "That's why I'm doing things like getting the iPads for the kids, so they can tell their own stories. This place looks a lot different depending on who's doing the telling." He put his mug down. "Probably every place does."

I thought again about the news report I'd seen in the hotel room in Churchill, and tried to recall what my reaction to it had been at the time. Which made me remember again, and want to ask about, the suicides. Not feeling able to, I looked around the trailer and noticed, for the first time, some bean bag chairs in a corner and a small plastic basketball hoop stuck to the wall.

A loud noise outside startled me as the front door opened and a man in a parka came in, stamped his feet, and closed the door. He pulled back his hood, revealing a shock of light brown hair spiked up at the edges from static electricity. Smoothing the stray hairs down, he looked around at us, smiled, and waved with the hand that wasn't messing with his hair. Then he locked eyes with Matt.

"Hey, I need to borrow your skidoo. Goin' ice fishing. Can I have the keys?"

Matt nodded and walked to a peg by the door where a coat was hanging. He reached into a pocket, pulled out the keys, and handed them to the man. "John, this is Samu from the sanctuary, and that's Lee, who's staying there." He turned to us. "This is John."

We said hello and he smiled again, then turned back to Matt, thanked him for the keys, and went back out the way he'd come in.

"What's a skidoo?" I asked Matt.

"Snowmobile."

"Will he bring it back before you need to go home?" Samu asked. "I can give you a ride if you want."

Matt shook his head. "Don't worry. I'll get home. It's a nice day."

Samu smiled. "Even with the polar bear?"

"Even with the polar bear."

Samu looked like he suddenly remembered something. "Hey, Matt, is that the John you were telling me about?"

"No, man, I was talking about my cousin John. This guy just moved back last year. I don't know him very well."

I could feel my eyebrows raise. "You don't know him very well but you gave him the keys to your snowmobile?"

"I'm not using it right now and he needs it. He'll probably bring me some fish later." Matt looked at me with an expression of mild amusement and went back to drinking his tea.

SHANNEN'S DREAM

No one spoke for a minute or two and I started to feel restless. I remembered Samu's comment about Matt working for Shannen's Dream and wondered if it had anything to do with the suicides.

"So what's Shannen's Dream?" I asked.

"Right. Sorry. Did I get side-tracked about something? That never happens." Matt looked sideways at Samu with a slight smirk. "It takes a little bit of explaining. Our elementary school was condemned after a diesel spill more than 20 years ago. The kids and teachers were all getting sick with breathing problems and rashes, but we couldn't afford to build a replacement. For non-Indigenous communities, educational money from Ottawa and Ontario is earmarked so it can't be used for anything else, right? But for First Nations, it all goes through the federal department for Indigenous affairs and some of it gets used for things like flood control and bureaucrats' salaries.

"So for almost a decade, our kids had to take classes in these little unconnected portable units without enough heat. Eventually, a thirteen-year-old girl named Shannen Koostachin learned that First Nations kids get less educational funding than other kids, and the years she spent trying to learn in those tiny cold units weren't just because of an accident. So she organized her classmates to tell their stories. They posted them on YouTube and Facebook, spoke to newspapers, at conferences, even organized a group of kids to go speak to Parliament."

"Wow. She kind of reminds me of my daughter," I said, looking into my mug. "Did she get the funding? What's she doing now?"

Matt studied me, sipping his tea. Samu said, "Unfortunately, Lee, Shannen died when she was fifteen. She and her sister went to New Liskeard so they could go to a better high school and she died in a car accident there."

I swallowed some of my tea the wrong way and started coughing uncontrollably. Samu patted my back a few times until I held up my hand to stop him.

He turned to Matt. "Lee's daughter also died."

Matt looked at me for a second and then back at his tea. "I'm sorry," he said, and he did look sorry. "To answer your question, Shannen's family and a lot of other people in the community continued where she left off. That's Shannen's Dream. Some teens even went to the UN in Geneva with a complaint against Canada. And they did get the funding for the school. It was built a few years after Shannen died... DC Comics even modeled a superhero on Shannen— Equinox, a Cree teenager with superpowers based on the seasons." He laughed.

"Really?" I asked. "That's amazing."

"Yeah, it's a good thing," Matt said, but didn't sound entirely convinced. "Representation's important. Why shouldn't there be Cree superheroes? But in Shannen's case, I think it also misses part of the point. Shannen came out of the community. She was a force of nature, but she didn't do what she did alone. All her classmates helped, and so did her parents, her family, and eventually First Nations kids all across Canada. Superheroes are individuals who swoop in and save other people who can't help themselves, right? They're exceptional by definition. Not really reflective of what an entire community can accomplish. Shannen was as amazing as any superhero, but it was her community that gave her strength and helped her succeed at what she did, and she was the first to say that."

Even as I considered this, nodding, my mind kept returning to the car accident. "What happened to her parents?" I asked, a little abruptly.

Matt looked like he didn't understand the question. "What do you mean what happened to them?"

"How did they cope with her death?"

"They continued her work," he answered, a little incredulously, as though I'd asked a question with an obvious answer. He looked at me more closely. "You said she reminds you of your daughter. What was your daughter like?"

I took a deep breath and suddenly had the sensation that I was looking at Matt and Samu through some kind of thick glass, like I was seeing them across a fish tank. I blinked. "My daughter was an activist too. She didn't start an organization or anything like that, but she did a lot of work on the U.S. border with Mexico, helping migrants who were crossing the desert." I could feel my heart beating against my clothes. "It's how she died. Or, at least, it's where she died." I wasn't drinking my tea anymore, just holding it. I put it down on the table and let my hand fall, and suddenly felt Ring's tongue on my knuckles. He'd situated himself under the table and hadn't made a sound or motion until now. I'd almost forgotten he was there.

Matt was still watching me. "Is anyone continuing her work?"

"What?"

"Her work. Her legacy," he repeated. "What are people doing to make sure it keeps going?"

"Oh… she was part of a group down there, VIDA. I assume they're still doing what she was doing…" I trailed off, trying to think of when I'd last heard about VIDA, if I'd heard anything at all since Rachel's death other than the information we had to get from them about her last days. I didn't blame them the way Susan seemed to, but thinking about them was painful. It hadn't occurred to me to wonder what they were currently doing or to think of the organization as having anything to do with Rachel anymore.

Samu cleared his throat. "Matt!" he said with too much energy. "I haven't told you why we need your help!" He reached under the table to pet Ring and coaxed him to come out into the open. My stomach dropped.

"This is Ring. He came to the sanctuary with a guest, Robert, who died unexpectedly of a heart attack." Matt looked at Samu skeptically. Samu shook his head. "No, really, he did have cancer, but he died unexpectedly of a heart attack and he left his dog with us. We can't keep him. I was hoping you might be able to get him on the next transport, maybe keep him at your house until then? We can pay for his food and everything." Samu looked hopeful.

Matt immediately shook his head. "No, man, the next transport isn't for weeks. It's not even scheduled yet. I can't keep him until then. My sister'll throw me out if I bring another dog home. We've already got four people living at her place, and she knows you've got all that space out there, so there's no way I could convince her this dog needs to stay in her home. I'm feeding about twenty dogs now. If I could bring in another dog, I'd bring in one of those. Anyways."

Matt patted his thigh and made a kind of clicking noise at Ring, who responded by walking over to him and leaning against his legs. "He's a nice dog, though. How old?"

Samu looked at me. "He's nine," I answered.

"Nine's old for a dog his size," Matt said. "He may not have more than a few years left. It'll be hard to find him a home. I usually send puppies and young dogs to the rescue because they get adopted faster. I don't tend to send them old dogs. Maybe they'd find him a home—who knows? He's sweet. But in the time it takes to place an old dog, they could take two or three younger ones from me."

"Are they the only rescue in Winnipeg?" Samu asked.

Matt sighed. "No, there's two, and there's also a shelter, but I don't think you want to send him to a shelter at his age. The guy didn't have any family to take him?"

Samu shook his head. "Can you talk to the rescue for us, see what they say? If they'll take him, we can pay to fly him to Winnipeg."

"Sure," Matt said, collecting our mugs. "And I tell you what. If they say okay, I'll come out to the sanctuary and get him. I haven't visited in a long time. We can go snowshoeing. I'll pick up some more vegetables." He winked.

Samu smiled and said, "Sounds like a plan," and we stood up to leave. The two men nodded at each other, and Matt showed us to the door. I thanked him for the tea. He smiled and said he had a feeling we'd have a chance to talk again.

As Samu loaded Ring onto the sled, I asked him, just to be sure, if the three of us were all going back to the sanctuary.

"Yes, of course," he replied. "Right now, we can't do anything else."

The reprieve opened up my lungs, and the air came rushing in.

LIGHTS

That night, I sat with Ring and Viviana on the platform, waiting for the lights. Wrapped in foil blankets, Ring all the way underneath mine and leaning against my legs, we were silent for a long time.

"What are you planning to do about Ring?" Viviana asked.

"Take care of him, for now," I said. "I don't have any other answers. I don't know if the rescue will take him or not."

"You know, you could decide not to walk the pillars and just adopt him."

"No," I said quietly. "I can't just take him back to Wisconsin. I have nothing to return to."

"He could be something to return to."

I didn't answer for some time.

"Viviana, is there anything that would make you not walk the pillars?"

She put her chin, hidden by the parka hood, into her gloved hands and leaned them against her knees, which were covered by the blanket. She started bouncing her legs a little, like she was restless.

"I don't know. Because I don't know if I'm walking them to begin with. I came here with no assumptions. I just wanted to be somewhere clean, somewhere empty, somewhere I could work on this while knowing there's an out if I can't take it. So the answer is, I guess, maybe. But I don't think it's anything on the outside that would change my mind. It would come from me, that I feel able to leave. That's all." She was now holding her knees though the foil and rocking her whole body back and forth.

"Does that help?"

"What?"

"The rocking."

"Yeah. Try it."

I grabbed my knees and tried to rock myself, but my right foot was underneath Ring, who protested when I moved.

"Is it some kind of nervous system thing?"

Viviana shrugged. "I think it's a body memory of being rocked by your mama."

"I don't think I was ever rocked by my mother. Or anyone. I don't remember my mother holding me, ever. I don't even remember her hugging me."

Viviana stopped rocking. "I don't think I've ever heard anyone say that. What does that mean? Did she abuse you?"

"Not anything obvious or physical, no. She just never hugged me or held me. She was, you know... cold... I hate using that term for any mother, including my own, given how they blame cold women for everything that happens to kids. My dad was there too until I was ten and I don't remember him ever hugging me either. I promised Rachel when she was born that she would never be able to say that. I held her all the time. Susan nursed her, but in between, I pretty much had her in a sling whenever I was home. She never wanted to be put down. Couldn't fall asleep, either, unless she was on one of us..." Now, despite his protests, I pulled my foot out from under Ring and began rocking myself, holding my knees.

"Where did you and Susan meet?" Viviana asked. This surprised me.

"College, in a French Lit class."

"What's she like?"

Again the images of Susan with her face drawn, her fingers gripping my sides, were what came to mind. I opened my mouth and then closed it again.

"Sorry," Viviana offered. "We don't need to talk about her."

"No, it's okay. I just have trouble thinking about her without fixating on the last year like it's the only time we had together. I know that isn't fair. When we met, we were so young. She had this long curly blond hair, wore skirts, flirted incessantly. She sought me out, and by the second week of the semester, I was living in her dorm room."

"Typical," Viviana said, laughing a little. "My girlfriend Joy and I moved in together quickly too. Couple of tours to Iraq took care of that, though."

Now I was sorry. "The stress of separation? Or... what happened to you?"

"No, it was before that. It was just a long time to be gone. And I could never promise it was the last time. Funny thing is, now I can promise I'm not going back. What happened with your wife?"

"We were never very similar. Even early on. I think the attraction may have been how different we were. But after Rachel was born, the differences became harder to square away or laugh at. We agreed on a lot about parenting. Rachel sleeping with us in bed as a baby, Susan nursing her into her toddler years and taking off from work until Rachel started school. I'd give her a breather after work and on weekends, taking Rachel on long walks, holding her at night when she had trouble sleeping. It's true I wasn't there all day with Rachel, and that I probably couldn't fully understand Susan's exhaustion from birthing and nursing her, from being the one to feed her breakfast, clean up her toys all day, take her to Mommy and Me classes and all that stuff.

"And maybe that was part of what made the gulf between us open a bit wider every year. She was just so afraid all the time; every stumble made her gasp or scream. It drove me crazy. Teaching Rachel to ride a bike, she acted like we were dropping her in a snake pit to fend for herself. She insisted we each hold one side of the bike and run with her; then she didn't want the training wheels to come off. Rachel and I constantly rolled our eyes behind Susan's back, probably starting at way too young an age. I felt like I was Rachel's accomplice in finding her freedom, her ability to do things, take risks. Maybe that went too far."

Ring shifted, so I started rocking back and forth more.

"Helping?"

"Not sure. Don't think so."

We were both quiet for a while, looking up at the sky.

"What if I rock you?" Viviana asked quietly.

"What?"

"What if I rock you? Maybe that would help."

"How?"

"On my lap. You don't look like you weigh much."

"But…" I looked at Viviana, but between the dark night and her parka hood, I could not discern her expression. "But…"

"What?"

"You don't like to be touched."

"I don't like to be touched without having control over it. That doesn't mean I can't have any physical contact. Plus we're in parkas."

I stopped rocking and stared at the floor of the platform.

"Lee, you can pretend I didn't offer that, but I gotta say, it seems like you yourself don't want to be touched. I've been surprised seeing you with Ring, because otherwise you look all contracted, like you don't want to be near anyone. I certainly understand that and would be the last person to criticize you for it, and it's fine to just forget my suggestion. But don't say it's because it would upset me. Offering comfort doesn't upset me. It kind of helps me."

I couldn't imagine. It was too strange, too intimate.

"When's the last time you had physical human contact?" Viviana asked.

"I don't know…. other than holding onto Samu on the snowmobile, or you cutting my hair?"

"Yeah, other than that."

"I don't know. Five months? Six? When I think about it, I just want to hold Rachel." I felt tears welling up and closed my eyes, trying to hold them back.

"Hey, haven't you been listening to Catherine and Samu? If you need to cry, cry. It's energy that needs to move out of you. Don't hold it back like that, especially not for me. You think I don't cry? Just let it out. It's okay. You need to do it."

I clenched my jaw.

"Lee, let's tap," Viviana said and turned to face me.

"With these gloves on?!" I looked at her.

"Sure, with the gloves on. It doesn't have to be so exact." She started tapping the inner eyebrow point. "Just tap. Here, follow me. We don't need to say anything. Just let yourself feel the crying coming up and tap to it. I'll close my eyes if you want." And she did.

I tapped, following Viviana's motions, trying to feel what she told me to feel, but my whole body clenched against it. "I don't think I actually need to…" And then it broke, and came out of me, though it was not crying as

I'd ever heard crying, but more of a kind of gasping sob, without tears and like I couldn't breathe. I stopped tapping and tried to catch my breath, and then the tears came, and I let them. I grabbed my knees again and rocked, sobbing, and then without meaning to, I leaned over onto Viviana's shoulder, wailing.

Realizing what I'd done, I started to pull back sharply, trying to apologize but unable to make any intelligible sound or stop the cries. As I pulled back, Viviana pulled me forward, until my head and shoulders were against her chest, my legs still on the platform floor. Slowly, almost imperceptibly, she started to rock. In spite of myself, I cried harder, feeling the safety of her arms around me, rocking.

"Rachel!" I sobbed, shaking, convulsing against Viviana's padded coat.

"You're the baby now," Viviana whispered. "You're the baby now, it's okay, just cry, you're the baby now, it's okay, just cry," she repeated, over and over. "Now she gets to hold you, because she's okay now, she can hold you now, it's okay, just cry, she's holding you now, just cry…"

As I sobbed, Ring pushed his way out from under the blanket and climbed onto Viviana's leg in order to reach my face and lick it. And he kept licking, warming the skin around my eyes with his tongue. I felt like I was suffocating, between his mouth on my face and Viviana's arms around me and all the clothes. And yet it was calming, the pressure of her arms, the insistence of Ring's tongue until I reached out and held him the way Viviana held me, and rocked him as she rocked me. Until I was able to speak again.

"Do you think the lights will come?" I asked.

"I do," she said.

SNOWSHOES

After months in bed, I had very little muscle left and even less endurance. Catherine made clear to me that even if I wanted to walk the pillars, I was in no shape to do so and would likely get no farther than Robert did. The prescription? Daily snowshoe hikes with Samu.

Ring, of course, tagged along, wearing his red paw coverings and his red coat, so light on his feet that he often stayed on the icy crust of the snow. In softer drifts, his legs fell through and he sometimes had to bound up and forward in a manner that made him look like a jackrabbit.

Samu outfitted me with glacier goggles to protect my eyes and the largest, widest snowshoes I'd ever seen. But they were made of aluminum and were light—so light I could barely tell I was lifting anything as I stepped.

For three days in a row, we took morning walks around the property. I knew I was weak, but the degree of my debilitation shocked me. For someone who had once been a runner, I now tired to the point of breathlessness from a quarter-mile of snowshoeing. In my cold showers in the morning, I started looking at my body and found it was alien, thin and bony with no discernible muscle tone. I bent my arm to look at my flexed bicep—something that delighted Rachel when she was little—only to see a small flaccid mound attached to my arm bone.

On the fourth day, we ventured out across the snow, Samu cutting the trail ahead of me, Ring tiptoeing or bounding behind me depending on the snow's consistency.

In the afternoons, I had a new vocation: ice baths. Samu taught me more of the Iceman's routines, including how to warm my freezing body by standing in "horse stance"—a wide stance with my legs in a partial squat—and breathing with a particular rhythm and energy flow while "pushing" the energy with my hands.

When I was ready, I lowered myself into a tub in the greenhouse filled with snow water and ice. Catherine stayed with me as the breath was pulled out of me by the cold. As I panicked, she bent over and spoke calmly in my ear, reminding me that after thirty seconds, I'd be able to breathe again, and to just count and wait for it, not to focus on the fear of losing my breath but to realize that I was, in fact, breathing and would continue to do so as my body adjusted.

And it did adjust. After two minutes, Catherine helped me out and firmly ordered me into horse stance and the warming routine which, to my surprise, brought the blood back into my limbs.

Once I was dressed and inside the lodge, a feeling of calm energy suffused me, a feeling that, at another point in my life, I might have labeled elation. I was not elated. But I was there, I was vital and, for a few minutes, aware only of the sensations in my body, I was OK.

Dog Food

I dreamed Ring was inside the frame of a painting. It was a painting with a thick natural wood frame, a simple painting almost like a child's, perhaps a child with talent. There was a bright green field, two trees, a blue sky with three clouds, and a shining sun. In the upper right corner was a big red barn and in the lower left corner was Ring, barely inside the frame, just starting to run. His front paws were slightly in the air and he was looking toward the barn and trying to get there, but he was frozen in place. I was standing in front of the painting with a bag of dog food in one hand and a few pieces of it in the other, holding the pieces out to the picture. "You need to eat before you go!" I kept repeating, over and over, to his miniature form inside the frame, poised to run but not running. Standing still in mid-air.

I woke with a light sweat on my face, confused until I realized it was pressed against Ring's back. He was awake but not moving, just staring at the wall. I began petting his side slowly, my hand starting at his head and moving down his back, then repeating. Eventually, he leaned his head back and licked my hand. Then he stretched his front legs with a groan, sat up, and shook himself. This was the sign to get up. I wasn't ready, but I followed his lead.

We were still in Robert's room. We slept there, and I fed Ring there and, in the mornings, we went to my room to get my clothes, towel, parka, and boots before starting the day.

Dipping my hand into the bag of food this morning, I realized that it wouldn't last much longer. There was still no plan for Ring, but he would continue to need to eat. I remembered Catherine telling me that Robert had to order the food to be flown into Attawapiskat, something both expensive and difficult. I would have to try to arrange a delivery. Yet I was afraid to even mention it, for fear that raising the subject would speed the process of them sending Ring to Winnipeg.

I fed Ring and left with him for the sauna.

Later in the day, I raised the issue of dog food with Catherine.

"Is it possible to get regular dog food for him in Attawapiskat?" I asked.

"No meat at the sanctuary. I'm sorry."

"Can you give me the information for ordering the food Robert got him and I'll order it and pay for it? If I can use the satellite phone?" I asked.

Catherine hesitated.

"I know you're looking for a place for him to go, but can he stay with me another couple of weeks? He's been through so much, he's just gotten back to eating a normal amount of food, and he's grown attached to me."

"You think it will be easier for him to leave if he stays longer and grows more attached to you?" Catherine asked skeptically.

I did not have an answer to that, so I didn't offer one.

"Lee, are you sure you're not asking for yourself? Because it's okay if you are."

"Will you let him stay a couple of weeks for me?" I asked.

"I will," she nodded. "It doesn't seem like we'll be able to find a place for him before then anyway. But if you feel something, it helps to acknowledge that you feel it. There's no penalty for having an emotion or desire, or for expressing it."

Maybe I looked unsure.

"You need to let what you're feeling move up and out of you more than you're doing. I think we should start myofascial release."

"What's that?"

Catherine told me that fascia are membranes like saran wrap that connect all our organs, ligaments, muscles, even bones. Myofascial release, she explained, is a kind of body work involving prolonged pressure on certain areas of the body to release the fascia. It was my last daily practice, and she was a trained practitioner.

"We don't start with it because it's intense and requires physical contact. You can decline if you want, but it's very powerful. We hold stored emotion in our fascia, and they bind together, holding it in. Myofascial release doesn't just help the body. It releases the emotions."

PRESSURE

I was lying on a table in my underwear, covered with a sheet. The table was set up in the small room off the hallway to the kitchen, at the end past the bedrooms. It was the size of a walk-in closet and perhaps was built as one. The table was the only thing in the space.

Catherine was standing next to me with her hands on the top of my chest, above my breast and where my other breast would be. She was pressing down with both hands and also gently pulling them away from each other, until I felt a pulling sensation that moved up into my neck and, oddly, down into my groin though her hands were nowhere near there. I expressed confusion.

"Just pay attention to it and accept how it feels. Give it the attention it wants," Catherine said. "All your fascia is connected. Releasing it in one area is like pulling the end of a tangled thread. You don't know where the other end is until you feel it."

After several minutes of pressure in the same spot, I suddenly realized I was in a partial dream state, unsure if I was asleep or awake. My eyes were closed, and I periodically found myself in other places—outside in the snow, on Robert's bed, in the old apartment, at Rachel's elementary school. When I'd realize it, I would suddenly be back on the table. Unsure what was happening, I asked Catherine, but she told me it was okay, just to go wherever it took me, that it was emotional energy being released.

She then moved to my jaw, which was uncomfortable and felt like she was pulling at my face. Though the sensation was intense, I drifted in and out even more, seeing shapes floating before me, arguing with Susan, crawling under a bed somewhere I didn't recognize. And then, unexpectedly, I cried out— unsure why, but waking myself in the process—and then the sound came again and it tipped into sobs.

"Just let it out. That's good," said Catherine. "It's energy—old energy. Let it out, let it out of your body."

But then it was gone, and I was awake, and the session was over.

SUSAN

Catherine had given me the satellite phone to order the food, which I did.

And then, as I sat in the office holding the phone, I thought of Susan.

We'd been married twenty-six years. I tried to get that number to mean something, but it just seemed large the way random numbers seem large, the way Rachel, when she was a kid, used to say any big quantity was "a thousand." A thousand socks, a thousand pieces of spaghetti, a thousand kisses. I guess I was married to Susan a thousand years. Not legally, of course—back then, I'd had to do a second parent adoption to even be recognized as Rachel's mother, which I was at the time—but married twenty-six years nonetheless, wedding in the park and all. Legally just under four years, with Rachel old enough to be our maid of honor when we went to city hall.

Part of the reason it seemed like a thousand years was that it had become—the marriage—just grooves in old wood, patterns we'd never seen ourselves falling into but did anyway. She said I was shut down. She, who could have used some shutting down herself. Her anxiety was increasing every year until every sound in the apartment set her off. She called Rachel mercilessly every day, or emailed, and sometimes emailed and then called her to tell her to read her email. It was if she didn't remember being twenty. She wasn't amused when I said, "Thank god our parents didn't have email when we were in college."

When they found Rachel, there was no time to even process anything. We were on the plane, we were at the morgue, and Susan was screaming and wailing nonstop, falling on the floor, incoherent. She wanted Rachel's body flown home but she didn't want it embalmed. Said Jews don't embalm, as if Rachel had ever cared about what Jews do or don't do. They wouldn't fly her without embalming her and this, for Susan, was a crisis. Our daughter was dead and it was a crisis whether they put formaldehyde in her body. I told them to do it, and then it was me she was screaming at. Suddenly, I was a goy with no understanding of what needed to be done, and I was bewildered and silent and told them just do it, it has to be done, we're not burying her down here.

And Susan insisted on putting her in the ground within forty-eight hours—Jewish law again, though she hadn't been to temple in decades and she herself had considered being cremated. But all of a sudden, the worst thing that ever happened had to be controlled by Jewish law, and while we could still barely breathe, or tell anyone, she needed to put our baby girl in the ground. Because Rachel was embalmed, I didn't understand why we couldn't wait. I wasn't ready, would never be ready, but certainly not ready the day we flew her body back and, my god, who does that? Jews, I was told, and was reminded that I wasn't one.

After the funeral, Susan wanted everyone to come back to the apartment to sit shiva. I just wanted to go to bed, but for seven days people were there, in and out of every room, even our bedroom, talking and whispering and insisting we eat. Within an hour after the burial, I was in bed, which infuriated her. Our daughter was dead, but my climbing into bed enraged her. Susan's aunts and uncles, second and third cousins, people I hardly knew, knocked on the door, and even though I never responded, they would open it and offer me food.

Her relatives came one by one and sat on the end of the bed with me laying in it, and tried to talk to me. It was unbelievable. We had just lost our daughter, our lives were gone, upside down, and she needed people she hadn't seen in years, people she had never liked, sitting in our apartment for days on end and entering the bedroom without invitation. She kept telling me Rachel was Jewish, as if this were news to me. Rachel hadn't entered a synagogue since her Bat Mitzvah.

And yet.

And yet a thousand years.

I dialed the phone. I felt ice surging up behind my breastbone, but I dialed. Her voice mail answered. She might have been looking at the phone as it rang and just not answered. It didn't mean anything because it wasn't my phone number and she wouldn't have recognized it. But it felt like something final.

"It's me," I said to the voice mail. "I just wanted you to know I'm okay. I'm in Canada visiting a friend. I'm going to stay a while. We're visiting a place up north and there's no cell service or internet, so I'm not reachable, just borrowing a satellite phone. I just don't want you to worry. I… I just… needed to come up here. And… I quit my job but I think you know that—I think Carol told you. I didn't want to just keep extending the leave, they needed to hire someone and… I really hope you're finding some way to… get through this and… I don't know that I can go back. So… I'm here and… I wanted to tell you that…. And that I'm sorry for everything. I just couldn't…. Please take care of yourself."

Afterward, I sat looking at the phone for a long time. It was oblong and heavy, like early cell phones, and the way it was silent and dumb, just seconds after conveying sounds and vibrations, seemed very much like our marriage.

The Morning After

When I got to the kitchen the next morning, Catherine was there making her drink. She smiled at me for a second and then bit her lip, like she was considering whether or not to tell me something. I waited, but when she just kept looking at me, I grew uncomfortable.

"Did something happen?" I asked.

"No. Well, yes, I guess. When I checked the phone this morning, there was a message from Susan. She'd really like to talk to you."

I felt a pit in my stomach, and my breathing constricted almost like at the beginning of the ice bath.

I cleared my throat. "I'm sorry I didn't tell you, but I left her a voice mail yesterday when I borrowed the phone. She must have seen the number. I know the phone's expensive and I'll pay for whatever time my message and hers took up."

"No, it's not that," Catherine replied, looking like she felt badly for making me think it was a problem. "It's just that I think maybe you should call her back."

I was quiet, trying to process that.

"Lee, you've been here for weeks. I could tell from her message that she doesn't even know where you are. I understand that you didn't want to tell her everything you were doing, everything you were planning, and that's your prerogative. But her message sounded almost hysterical with worry."

"That's her natural state," I offered. Catherine looked taken aback by this comment, and I realized it must have seemed extraordinarily cold, given the circumstances.

"We've been through a lot," I conceded. "We just don't communicate very well anymore. I'm not sure my calling her would make her feel any less hysterical."

Catherine considered this for a few moments. "Well, I can't tell you what to do. You obviously don't have to call her back. But personally, I don't think this is about a breakdown in communication. I think that, to some extent, you're just avoiding feeling whatever talking to her makes you feel. And since you called her yesterday and couldn't have been sure she wouldn't pick up, it seems like a part of you wants to talk to her. How long were you together?"

"About thirty years. We were married for twenty-six. I guess technically we still are."

"That's a long time. And she's Rachel's other parent. She's possibly the only person who truly understands what you're going through."

I felt nauseous, like I might throw up. I swallowed hard and waited for the feeling to subside before answering. "She actually doesn't understand what I'm going through. She's going through something different than I am. All she'd want to talk about is the investigation. That and how she can't understand the way I act, and the degree to which I'm disappointing her."

"Okay. But, after thirty years and losing a child, don't you think you could at least give her some sense of where you are and that, for now, you're physically okay? Rachel disappeared and then was found dead, and neither of you knows what happened to her. Other than Rachel, you've been the person closest to Susan. Did it ever occur to you that just disappearing like you did, with only vague information about where you were going, might make her feel like it's happening all over again?"

No. It seemed unbelievable now, but I had not considered it in that way. My existence in Madison hadn't seemed to be helping Susan. If anything, I'd felt like a burden to her, like someone she still felt responsible for when she didn't want to be. And, as anxious as Susan was, she seemed much more functional than me at this point, had gone back to work, had managed an investigation that, while consistently unsuccessful, still required a lot of thought and organization. She was the one who left first, and we hadn't talked much since, mostly communicating necessary information through Jenna, Carol, and her other friends when they stopped by to check on me.

She seemed to be getting through her days and talking to other people, so I hadn't thought much about how my actions might affect her. I'd only considered what I needed, because I needed it so badly. I couldn't handle staying, couldn't handle our communications, couldn't handle being alive, so

I'd done what I felt I had to do. I guess when I thought of our relationship, I just thought of our paths having diverged, like a fork in the road. Like that old Robert Frost poem. She went in one direction and I went in the other.

I hadn't considered that the manner in which I left, and the degree to which I stopped communicating, might seem like a replay of some sort. Which, of course, begged the question of what my actually walking might do to her. At this thought, my mind shut down, was wiped blank. The train of thought just left my head like a stunned bird taking flight, and I stood there facing Catherine, thoughtless and dumb.

She looked at me sympathetically. "Well, if you want to talk to her, you're free to use the phone." She turned around and stretched her hand toward the counter, and I saw that she was reaching for it. She had brought it to the kitchen with her, having assumed that I would make the call.

My mind was still blank, but I found myself reaching my hand out to accept the phone from her. I wasn't sure what to do, so I just stood there looking at it.

"You can use the office if you want privacy," Catherine offered. I turned around and, not quite knowing where my feet were taking me, walked to the office, Ring trailing behind.

LEGACY

When Susan answered, my stomach seized up. She had to say "hello?" twice more, and still I couldn't think of what to say.

"Lee? Is that you? Will you please say something?" she said in a voice that was half whisper, half sob. "Lee!"

"Hey, I'm so sorry I didn't call before yesterday. I really am. I've just been... trying to get through each day."

Now Susan sounded tense, bordering on exasperated—a tone of voice I knew well. "Do you have any idea how worried I've been? Canada?! What friend? What friend do you have in Canada? Where are you, really?"

"Please try to calm down. I really am in Canada. I really did come to see a friend." I wasn't used to lying, especially to her, and I couldn't tell how convincing I sounded.

"What friend, Lee? Who do you know in Canada? You've hardly had any friends of your own for twenty years. I know practically every person you've spoken to since we were in college. What friend?"

A familiar sense of panic and speechlessness set in. It was always hard for me to argue with Susan, and much more so when I wasn't telling the truth. "Luz," I lied again. "Luz, who used to work in the development office with me. Remember she got married and moved to Canada?" She had moved to Toronto, but I was hoping Susan wouldn't remember this detail. What she probably did remember was that Luz and I had never been close enough to spend weeks together.

"You've barely gotten out of bed or talked to anyone for months, but you flew to Canada to see an old colleague?" She was incredulous.

"I visited her for a little bit, and then we came north to… stay at a yoga retreat. She went home, but I decided to stay here for a while longer. Maybe permanently."

"A yoga retreat?? You? Now? What the fuck, Lee? You really think I believe you're doing yoga?"

Now, at least, I could be honest. "I'm absolutely doing yoga. Every day. It's helping a little. I'm doing breathing exercises and going snowshoeing. Seriously. I'm not in bed most of the time anymore. I thought you'd want to know that."

She was silent for a moment, and when she answered, she sounded calmer. "I can't believe it," she said quietly. But her tone sounded, finally, like she did believe me. "Where in Canada are you?"

I swallowed. "James Bay."

"James Bay?" she asked, and then, when I didn't respond in any way, she was silent. I knew she was remembering the trip that Rachel and I had planned, and that somehow this would make it fall more into place for her.

So I continued. "I'm not sure I can go back anytime soon. There's something about the snow up here, and the light, and being in a place like this. It feels like all I can do right now. It feels separate from everything else. I just need to stay for a while."

She sighed audibly, but "OK" was all she said. In our silence, I could hear small crackling sounds through the receiver.

"Susan, have you ever thought about a legacy for Rachel?"

"What?"

"A legacy," I said. "Something to carry on in her name."

"The investigation was carried on in her name. Who do you think that was for? I've tried to get justice for her. You've done almost nothing to help me." I could hear her anger rising. I knew the facial expression that went with that tone of voice and could see it in my mind.

"I'm sorry," I said. "I really am. But that's not what I mean. What I'm trying to say is… I was thinking that maybe we should do something to continue the work she was doing. Maybe help the organization she was working for."

She emitted a sharp sob, almost like a gasp. "How can you say that?" she asked, her voice growing louder and higher pitched. "Help VIDA? They're why she's dead! How can you want to do anything for them?" She started to cry.

My heart was beating hard against my shirt, but I answered. "Not for them, but for the people they're trying to help, the people Rachel was trying to help. That's what she chose to do, what she cared about." I did not mean to start this argument again, about Rachel's choices, and tried to shut it down by rephrasing. "All I'm saying is, she really, really believed in it. It seems like she would have wanted—"

Susan started to interrupt me but, uncharacteristically, I raised my voice and cut her off. "Just listen to me for a second. Please?" For once, she stopped talking. "What I mean is, I'd like us to do something in her name. Start a fund of some kind to help continue the work she wanted to do. It can be with a different organization. It doesn't have to be VIDA. People would contribute. I was hoping you might have some ideas, might be willing to work on—"

"Lee," Susan's tone sounded almost cold now, but her voice was shaking. "I've been going to work, living in a new place, handling all the paperwork, going over the reports, trying to figure out what happened to our daughter, and I'm really just barely hanging on. If you don't think that's enough, if you think there's something else we should be doing, why don't you get off your ass and come back here and do it? You want to hide up in Canada and do yoga, and me to work on this idea you suddenly have? After you've done nothing for months? Really?"

"You're right," I said. I still didn't think she understood, but it was not lost on me that this was not the time, and I was not the person, to raise the idea with her. She was right that there was no rational reason for me to put this on her. I was in another country, not planning on ever going back and, unbeknownst to her, not even planning on staying alive, and yet I was asking her to do something just because I wanted to know it was being done. Just because it suddenly felt wrong to leave without ensuring Rachel's work would continue.

"My time's running out," I said, not letting her in on the irony of that statement. "It's a satellite phone and they only let me use it for a few minutes. It's normally just for business and emergencies. I… just didn't want you to worry so much."

"If you didn't want me to worry so much, you think maybe you could have let me know what you were doing, so I didn't have to get a call from Jenna telling me you left a two-sentence note on the door?"

"You're right," I said. "I'm sorry." She asked if I needed anything, and I said I didn't. There was another moment of silence and then, after we said goodbye with no mention of when we might speak again, I added, quickly and quietly, "I love you."

DAYS

Snowshoeing made me feel almost alive. We were going about a mile every day now, in the early afternoon when the sun was brightest. Pushing my legs forward, feeling them sink a little and lifting them up again, the way I'd be out of breath and feel sweat beading on my forehead under my hat and hood, the way the air hurt, the way the light streamed on the snow, the way I couldn't think or feel anything but the force of moving forward and the way it strained me, the way it spent my muscles, the way I felt my muscles without thinking, the way I was my muscles and my lungs, the way my lungs seemed to grow and fill my chest, fill my throat. The way it was just snow, unbroken, in front of us. The way we left prints behind us but couldn't see them until we turned around.

My days now took me from early morning to early evening, though every time I realized I had such a full schedule, it made me want to lie down. Each activity was doable if it was only the thing I was doing and nothing else. And then only the next thing. I would wake, feed Ring, then go to the sauna for hot cold. Then I'd make my green drink, and we'd move on to the greenhouse. Then meditation in the hut with Catherine, with Ring lying a few feet away, breathing audibly. Then snowshoeing with Samu, and then my ice bath, and lunch. The snowshoeing and ice bath made it easier to eat, and I found lunch was no longer a struggle.

After lunch, I tapped with Catherine in one of the training huts with Ring at my feet, and then did yoga and Iceman breathing exercises with Samu and Viviana in the lodge while Ring slept on a couch. Yoga was immediately followed by more meditation and meditative breathing with Catherine, and then cleaning tasks and chores in one of the hydroponic greenhouses. Then a myofascial release session before helping with dinner, feeding Ring, and eating.

After dinner, we sat by the fire in the lodge, after which Ring and I followed Viviana out to the platform to watch for the lights. Ring and I were normally in bed in Robert's room by seven, and I found myself falling into sleep more and more quickly, with fewer awakenings during the night.

Eventually, I proposed to Ring that we try my room for a night and, finding that we slept just as well, I moved his food in there.

I lost track of how long I'd been at the sanctuary. I settled into something with whatever was left of me. It felt like a slight thawing, except that word implies a re-emergence of something that was there all along, underneath, and I wasn't sure that's what was happening. I found the more I exhausted my body, the more I just sank down into whatever it felt and focused only on the activity at hand, the less I felt like I was trying to get through something. Sometimes, despite myself, there was only breath and sun and Ring by my side, or darkness and heat or cold, or breathing or tapping, or the sensation of Ring's breathing against my chest, the feel of his tongue on my hand.

Rachel was there, always, but as the backdrop to everything I did, as the person I explained it to at night, in my head, looking for the lights, as the presence always in the peripheral vision of my mind. If I tried to think ahead to Ring's departure or walking the pillars or even to the next activity of the day, the pressure and ache in my chest returned. But just as my breath returned after thirty seconds in the cold, making the cold bearable, I let the feeling move through me, and then it was gone.

Matt's unannounced arrival at the sanctuary took me by surprise.

SPECIAL DELIVERY

It was time for snowshoeing but Samu wasn't waiting for me in the usual spot, so I walked around the main building looking for him, eventually wandering into the lodge. He wasn't there either but, to my surprise, Matt was sitting in front of the wood stove, his boots off and parka strewn across the chair next to him. He was wiggling his toes in his socks and stretching his feet toward the fire, which was roaring.

I stopped short just inside the arch of the doorway, looking at him. He turned toward me.

"Special delivery!" he called out with a smile, and pointed to a huge bag of dry dog food and two cases of wet food on the floor by the door to the outside.

My heart started beating fast, and I reflexively pulled Ring against my legs. All I could think to say in response was "When did you get here?"

"About thirty minutes ago. Samu just went to get me some tea. I'm gonna join your snowshoe outing. After I warm up."

"Are you here to take Ring?" I still hadn't moved from the archway and could barely get the words out.

Matt shook his head and looked amused. "It wouldn't make a lot of sense for me to lug thirty pounds of dog food all the way out here if I'd come to take the dog, would it?" He winked.

I audibly breathed a sigh of relief, then felt embarrassed. As I walked over to join Matt by the fire, I felt Ring close behind. When I sat down, he walked over to Matt and sniffed his hand, then lay down next to his feet.

"So you came all the way out here just to deliver the dog food?" I realize that I hadn't considered how the food would get here once it arrived in Attawapiskat. Every trip into town took hours. "Does that mean the rescue won't take him?" I added, trying not to sound too hopeful, and failing.

"I didn't say that, eh. They may, eventually. But Catherine doesn't seem like she wants to wait that long, so I gave her the contact information for the shelter in Winnipeg and another rescue. I think she'll probably reach out to them."

I felt a familiar sinking feeling. We were both silent for a minute, staring at the fire, before I changed the subject.

"You came out on the ice road and then by snowmobile?"

"No other way to get here this time of year. I used the skidoo the whole way, since it's all I've got. I don't know if you noticed, but there's a groomed trail next to the road."

I shook my head. I hadn't noticed. "How long did it take you?"

"Less time than it took you, I imagine. I take no prisoners when I'm driving." He smiled.

"Before coming here, I'd never seen anything like the ice road. I think it's amazing, though to be honest, the cracks scare me a little. Is it hard to maintain?" My heart was still beating fast from thinking he was there for Ring. Even though I understood Matt wasn't taking him this time, I felt the need to steer the conversation somewhere else.

"We don't call it the ice road. We call it the winter road. Or Kimesskanemenow, which means 'our road.' Because it's built and maintained by the four nearest Nehiyawak nations— Attawapiskat, Kashechewan, Fort Albany, and Moosonee. And yeah, it's a lot of work. De Beers has been funding it for years because they use it to move fuel and equipment to the mines. But when the mine shuts down, we're hoping the federal government will take over funding some of it, since it hooks up to the Ontario highway system."

"Who's De Beers?" I remembered seeing the outline of the word on the side of Matt's trailer and thinking it sounded familiar. I'd meant to ask him or Samu about it, but it was hard for me to hold onto a question or thought for very long unless it had to do with Rachel or, I was realizing, Ring.

"The company that built and runs the Victor Diamond Mine. You don't know about the mine?" He looked surprised.

"I knew the road went out to a mine. But I didn't know who ran it, or what De Beers was."

"They didn't have those 'diamonds are forever' ads in the States when you were a kid?"

"Oh. Actually, I do remember those ads. I remember them because I hated them. They always had a man and woman getting engaged and the woman all breathless about getting a diamond like it was the highlight of her life. I just didn't remember the company's name."

"Well, that was De Beers. Bringing ethically challenged diamonds to the world since before I was born." He sighed.

"How long has the mine been here?"

"The Victor Mine? De Beers opened it in 2008. That's not what I meant by before I was born. You know anything about blood diamonds?"

"A little."

"De Beers isn't a Canadian company. It's mostly owned by a firm called—wait for it—Anglo American." Matt looked at me like he was waiting for a reaction.

I raised my eyebrows.

"It gets better, though," he said. "The other major shareholder is the government of Botswana."

"That's crazy."

"It is. The government of Botswana gets a share of the diamonds being mined from Attawapiskat's traditional land, and we don't. But if you know the history of De Beers, it's not surprising. They've been mining in Botswana, Namibia, and South Africa for a lot longer than they've been here. Child labor, forced labor, miners losing arms, the whole deal. Blood diamonds. So now they mine on Attawapiskat land and market the diamonds as blood-free. As in 'You can buy Canadian diamonds and avoid ethical concerns.' Unless, of course, you ask a few questions." Matt smiled a little. "Which most people don't."

I wasn't sure if he intended this last comment as an invitation to ask more questions, or as some sort of implication. I moved my chair closer to the fire.

Matt looked at me. "My sister complains that I never shut up about politics. She says sometimes we just need to focus on what's in front of us for the day and not constantly analyze everything. To me, it's all connected. It's part of what my daily life is about."

"No, I get that," I said. "And my daughter would have agreed with you, too. She felt the same way… So Attawapiskat doesn't get anything from the mine being there?"

Matt audibly blew air out through his nose. "I mean, some people got jobs there and were glad to have the work. And we negotiated some benefits. But the mine's not technically on the reserve, so Attawapiskat didn't have a right of refusal when it was built even though it's on our traditional land and a lot of people opposed it for environmental reasons. De Beers did have to consult with us because of what they're doing and how close to the reserve they are, so we were faced with either negotiating an Impact Benefit Agreement to try to get something for the community or outright opposing the mine and then likely watching it get built anyway without any benefit to us. So we negotiated and got what we could. They were supposed to give us a small portion of their profits, help with housing on the reserve, employ a lot of people. But you can probably imagine how that turned out."

At that moment, Samu came in with two mugs of tea. "Lee, there you are!" he said, handing us each a mug. "I didn't know you were in here. Here, take this. I'll go get myself another cup. Matt's going to go snowshoeing with us, which will be great. I'll be right back."

I turned back to Matt. "So the agreement wasn't that helpful?"

"Now why would you assume that, eh?" Matt smiled wryly. "Even though it's our traditional land, because we don't have legal control over it, the royalties go to the Ontario government, not to Attawapiskat. We did get something—don't get me wrong. About a million dollars a year. But you know how much the company brings in from the diamonds they extract from our territory? About four hundred million a year. So they were putting about a fourth of one percent of their revenue back into the community. Meanwhile, twenty-five percent of our housing was literally at the point of falling down and they were supposed to be helping with that, per the agreement."

I shook my head and we both sipped our tea. Matt continued.

"So at one point, a bunch of young people blocked the winter road, and after that, the contributions increased to two million a year and they shipped some new trailers up to us. Also a few of their old trailers—my office is in one of those. But it still wasn't enough to make a big difference. They gave jobs to about a hundred people, but now the mine's gonna close, so the jobs and the contributions, such as they are, will stop, as will the funding for the winter road. But the mess they've made of the land—that will remain. I guess that's what they mean by diamonds are forever, eh?"

I laughed a little and acknowledged that sounded like an accurate if unintended interpretation. And then an uncomfortable thought occurred to me.

"Matt, if the mine's on traditional Attawapiskat land, does that mean the sanctuary is too?" This whole time, I'd thought of the sanctuary as being on empty unpopulated land away from everything.

Matt stared at the fire and nodded. "Most of Canada's on someone's traditional land. It's not something settlers think about much."

At the word "settlers," I turned and looked at him, not entirely sure who he was referring to.

"Non-Indigenous Canadians." Matt smiled. "Sorry, and non-Indigenous Americans. Wasn't trying to exclude you."

Samu returned at that moment, carrying another mug and wearing a big smile. He pulled a chair up on Matt's other side and sat down.

"We were just talking about the mine," Matt said to Samu. "You're not a very good tour guide, eh. Lee didn't know anything about it." He winked.

"You're right," said Samu, looking at the fire. "But I have a lot of things to explain. I need to go by what each person can handle. And what they're interested in learning."

For the first time, I felt like Samu was trying to tell me something indirectly. I held my cup and looked at the fire, feeling a little taken aback. He was right, though. I hadn't shown much interest in the nearest community until now.

Matt and Samu sipped their tea, while Ring stretched his front legs closer to the stove and sighed.

SNOWCLONE

When we went outside, the sun was so bright that we had to put on snow goggles to protect our eyes from the reflection off the snow. Samu asked me if I thought I could handle a slightly longer walk, and I said I could. He took the lead, as usual, with Matt following behind him and then me.

As we left the courtyard and entered the wide-open space behind the sanctuary, Matt started pointing at things and trying to talk to me. I walked faster to try to catch up so I could hear.

"See that crusty snow over there? That's called watenikwan in Swampy Cree. And those windblown drifts over there? They're called piskwacistin." He was smiling like something was funny.

"I heard as a kid that the Inuit have a hundred words for snow!" I yelled back. "The Cree do also?"

I could hear Matt laughing loudly. He stopped and turned around to face me so that he didn't have to keep shouting. "How did I know you'd ask me that, eh?" He laughed hard again and put his gloved hand over his side, like he needed to physically contain the laughing, and it suddenly occurred to me that he'd set me up, that he'd been joking around, trying to catch me at something.

"First of all, there's no one Inuit language. There are many. And not one of them has a hundred words for snow. Second, those languages are what are called agglutinative languages, where words are made by combining different ideas. So the words you're talking about are kind of like compound words. They're made from putting two thoughts together, like snow and the way the particular snow looks or the way it fell. It's the same with Nehiyawak languages. Just a different way of using description, the way you might look at that and think 'that snow is crusty'—we just put the words together into one word."

He pushed his goggles up and wiped his eyes with the back of his glove, then pulled them back down. "I'm just poking fun. You don't have to look so embarrassed. It's just that the hundred words for snow thing is so pervasive, it has a name: 'snowclone.' It started with some white anthropologist almost a century ago and took off like a global game of telephone, with the number of words getting bigger and bigger."

"Got it," I said. "I won't ever ask anyone that again."

"If we did have a hundred words for snow, though, we'd have to come up with more now anyways. It's changing so much with the climate that we get all these weird weather events. The TV weather people keep coming up with new names for them: snowmageddon, bomb cyclone. I think we're gonna have to start asking if Canadian and American newscasters really have a hundred words for snow."

I realized I was smiling. I could feel the muscles in my face raising the corners of my mouth, and it felt almost painful, like it was straining the lower part of my face. But processing what he'd said, I realized I hadn't paid much attention to the climate here, only the weather on any given day.

"Have you noticed other changes from the climate?" I asked.

Matt stopped laughing and sighed. "Yeah, it's like a domino effect. It's changing almost everything. When and where the geese migrate, the kind of fish, even the plants. You've probably noticed how expensive it is to buy food up here. A lot of people hunt and fish to supplement, but it's getting harder. Geese are a big food source in the spring, but sometimes they don't even stop here now. Instead, we're seeing weird birds like pelicans, who never came here before. Talk to me in ten years, I guess. But so far, I'm not ready to start eating pelicans, eh."

He shook his head and continued. "Getting around is harder too, because the winter road season's shorter. I know this probably seems cold to you, but believe me, it used to get a lot colder. And the weather's just totally unpredictable now. We get thunderstorms in December. When I was growing up, I never saw rain in December, much less lightning and thunder. Sometimes, I can't tell what season it is when I wake up in the morning. It's a mess. Anyways." He scowled.

Samu finally noticed we'd stopped walking and was heading back toward us. "Hey!" he called out. "What's up?"

CONTAGION

During lunch, Catherine quizzed Matt about all the goings-on in town, since she rarely made the trip. How many new houses had been built, how the youth center was going, whether he'd heard anything about future funding for the winter road. Samu asked after Matt's family, and Matt said his nephew had a girlfriend, a smart kid who was a good influence on him.

I asked Matt how he came to live with his sister. He said he'd lived in Toronto for years after getting his degree, but when his brother-in-law died a decade ago, he moved back to help her raise her kids. They were now fourteen and seventeen, and were part of the reason he'd helped start the youth center. Viviana seemed to listen with interest but didn't say much.

As we were clearing the table, Samu asked Matt which kinds of vegetables he wanted to take back with him and whether his sister had made any special requests. Matt listed his preferences, and I volunteered to take him to the greenhouse and help him. On her way to the kitchen, Catherine looked back at me over her shoulder, clearly surprised I'd offered. But I had something I wanted to ask Matt, something I'd been thinking about since visiting him in Attawapiskat, maybe even since the hotel room in Churchill. Ring stayed in the lodge with Viviana while I walked out with Matt.

When we were alone in the greenhouse, me cutting kale and Matt picking green beans, I saw my chance.

"Matt, I was wondering if I can ask you something."

"Shoot!" he responded casually, not looking up from the vines.

"It's about the suicides in Attawapiskat."

Matt stopped what he was doing and looked up. He didn't say anything, just waited.

"I know it's gotten better and that the youth center is part of that, but I was wondering what else…" I suddenly wasn't entirely sure what I was asking, and Matt's silence indicated he wasn't either. It was more of a feeling, an emotional question mark, than a thought-out inquiry. There was something I needed to understand and didn't. "Why do you think it's been happening, and what else do you think would help and… how does the rest of the community… cope?"

Matt put down the pail he was holding and took a deep breath.

"That's a big question. Two or three big questions, actually."

"I know, I'm sorry. Please forget I asked." I realized I shouldn't have raised the subject so abruptly. But Matt didn't seem upset, just thoughtful.

"No, they're important questions. The answers are just complicated. Some people think it's just about poverty, or that bringing in more western-style mental health workers will fix it. And it's not like those things don't matter. The lack of resources is really hard, especially for some of the younger kids. They need more of everything—more and better housing so they can have some privacy and feel safe, better schools, more activities and things to do. They need better health care—when kids have diabetes and asthma and other illnesses, it puts a lot of stress on their emotional health, not just their physical health.

"So resources like that are part of it. And mental health care is important—suicide interventions and social workers and everything else." Now his voice sounded a little tight, tense. I could tell there was something else and stood still, waiting to hear the rest of his answer.

"But that's really not all the problems, and it's not all the solutions either. Our kids aren't just lacking resources. They're also dealing with colonialism and racism. Not personal interactions with settlers in their daily lives—they're lucky, in that way, not to live around many. But all the incursions into our sovereignty, the whole set-up of the educational system, the way money flows into or is withheld from the community, the way we're covered in the news and talked about on TV, the way they know what happened to most of our land. All that takes a toll."

He paused to take a breath, pushing back a strand of black hair that had escaped his ponytail. "We point out to Ottawa that we're underfunded compared to non-Indigenous communities, and the federal government responds by putting us in receivership—sends out some white guy to take over the Council's finances. What does that say to our kids? Some of the kids move away to go to better schools. What does that say to the ones who stay? Some get sent to boarding schools in other towns where they get bullied and abused, and then they carry that with them when they come back."

Some of the plastic sheeting on one of the greenhouse walls crinkled and briefly became convex as a small gust of wind pushed at it from the outside. Matt looked past me for a second, then continued. "There's also intergenerational trauma. Kids are more likely to attempt suicide if their parents or grandparents were forced to attend residential schools, regardless of what's happening in their own lives. So all of this combines together. But you know which one thing puts a person most at risk of attempting suicide?"

"No," I said, my stomach tightening. "What?"

"Knowing someone who died by suicide. That's the one biggest risk factor. Suicide's contagious."

"What do you mean, contagious?" The beating of my heart became noticeable and I felt a small bead of sweat on my forehead. I focused on my feet on the ground, on the breath entering my nostrils.

"When someone commits suicide, it tends to spur other people they know to attempt it too. If one person from an army unit kills themself, the risk increases for everyone else from that unit. If a parent kills themself, their child's more likely to try later on. And when one kid at Attawapiskat commits suicide, it increases the risk to all the other kids. Because it's a small place, they all know each other.

"It's partially the trauma of having it happen to a friend or family member, but it's also more than that. It's like some kind of permission, an idea that this is a way to solve problems, a removal of a social safeguard. The crisis got so bad partly because groups of kids were making pacts—five, eight, eleven at a time. And it just snowballed. Luckily, most of them didn't complete it. But, for weeks, the hospital waiting room was full with kids who tried. And it seemed like the medical air-lifts were constant for a while, for the ones who'd hurt themselves and needed more than the hospital here could do." He sighed. "Anyways." He stretched his arm out and reached for the pail.

There was something else I needed to know. "I'm really sorry to ask this. I know it sounds weird, but …." I could feel a lump growing in my throat. "Did they leave notes?"

Matt took his hand off the pail again and squinted at me, like he was trying to figure out why I would ask that. He didn't look angry or sad, just like there was something he didn't quite understand but was trying to.

"Most people who attempt don't leave notes. I don't think it means anything one way or another, whether they left a note."

I inhaled deeply and held my breath for a few seconds, trying to calm my heart. The absence of a note had always seemed so important. The detective had told us it didn't mean anything, but neither Susan nor I had believed that.

I didn't say anything at first, just stood there looking at the ground. But then, surprising myself, I told Matt. "My daughter didn't leave a note. The police thought she might have killed herself, but we were sure she didn't. That she wouldn't have. I still don't think she did. But maybe most parents feel that way . . . even when it's true." I felt my breathing get shallow and tried to inhale and exhale more slowly and deliberately. "I'm sorry. I don't mean to make this about me, about my daughter." That was a lie, and I knew it, and I knew that Matt knew it. "I guess that's not true. To me, everything's about my daughter. It's why I'm asking you these things. I'm sorry."

Matt looked at me silently for a few seconds, then nodded slowly. "I'm sorry for whatever happened. And I'm sorry you don't know. That can make it even harder."

"I don't really know how anything could make it easier. I don't know how anyone survives this."

"Other people."

"What do you mean?"

"People survive this by being around other people. By being with their community. By doing things to honor the memory."

I didn't really know how this applied to me. Our community, such as it was, might have helped Susan, but the only thing I'd wanted was to be left alone.

Matt continued. "You wanted to know what helps prevent suicides. Part of it's understanding about the contagion. That staying alive isn't just important for the person considering suicide—it's important for everyone who knows that person. Nehiyawak culture is big on community, our interconnectedness, our responsibility for each other. It helps, to some extent, for the kids who are having trouble to know that staying alive is a service to their community. Just staying alive. Even if that's all they do. Staying alive is a way to take care of their family, of the other kids, and especially the younger kids. That if they can just hang on, just not kill themselves, they're protecting their little brothers and sisters, their cousins, their friends, and their friends' little brothers and sisters and cousins."

This was not something I'd ever thought of. It made a certain kind of sense, and I wondered if it had anything to do with me, with my situation. If not knowing what happened to Rachel, whether she did something to herself purposefully, was part of what had led me here. If staying alive myself would be a service to anyone at this point. I didn't think so, though Susan's face kept intruding into my thoughts, and I tried to keep pushing it away.

"It's also helpful, in terms of suicide prevention, when the kids are able to reimagine what their lives mean, when they take on art and writing projects that focus on the beauty around them, their identity, their history, their community. It's important that they comprehend in a very fundamental way how amazing the generations before them were to survive everything they survived, to have kept our culture alive. This isn't something mental health workers shipped in from Timmins can help them with. It's something they learn by engaging with their community and environment, by creating projects and making art to reflect on the connections. Some of our teens have made truly remarkable art projects, film projects, community walks. If there were internet service here, I'd show you some of it. It's amazing."

"Art projects really help that much? When my daughter was young, she used to make up songs on the piano when she got upset, to self-soothe. Do you think that's what the art does? Helps the kids self-soothe?"

Matt had looked like he was going to start picking again, but he turned back to me. "It's not just the art, it's the process of purposefully looking around their environment and reinterpreting it, celebrating it, defining it on their own terms." He looked pensive. "There's been research showing that the Indigenous kids who participate most in traditional skill building, rituals, ceremonies, language—those are the kids least likely to try to take their own lives. Nehiyawak have survived so much and we're still here—we have culture, humor, a connection to our land. Our kids can see that better when they take part in the activities and ceremonies their ancestors participated in, when they can tie their own identity to the past generations, see the meaning and the continuity, how they belong. And then translate all of that into their own experiences, their own projects."

He was nodding now and picked up the pail again. "So the youth center helps with that, gives the kids the space and support to do these things. Speaking Nehiyawak, involving the elders. That doesn't mean we don't need equitable funding, better housing and health care, social work, schools, and all the rest. Our kids need all the same things other kids need. It's just also not enough after everything our community's been through. There's pieces of this that only we can do for ourselves. We sometimes talk about that like it's unique to Indigenous kids, but I actually don't think it is. Everyone needs community and identity, especially if history has done its best to rip yours apart."

I looked down, wondering who Rachel considered her community, if we'd done enough to create one for her growing up. I didn't have much to transfer to her. She had a little bit of Jewish community, the temple we belonged to when she was young and went to Hebrew school, and Susan's extended family. But it wasn't central for Rachel, and after her Bat Mitzvah, she moved on to other things.

There were other queer families in town, but we mostly interacted when the kids were small—playdates and outings. Rachel outgrew that too. Moved on to her own friends and interests, until we saw the other families only sporadically. As she grew up, she always had friends, but I didn't know if that meant she had community, and I wasn't sure what she saw as her identity. I wondered if the work she did on the border, to some extent, was an attempt to find that, if her colleagues served as a kind of community for her.

I thought, too, that as Rachel had moved on to her own interests, I'd lost touch with people myself. It hadn't seemed like a big deal at the time. But between parenting and work and something else I couldn't really put my finger on, my friendships had just sort of disappeared.

Matt seemed to notice my silence, though he couldn't have known what

I was thinking. He looked at me, and when he spoke again, it was slowly and intentionally. "It's important for the kids, and the adults too, to understand that none of us are defined by the worst things that happen to us, the worst things other people do to us. We're all a lot more than that."

I wasn't sure that was true. I didn't feel like a lot more than the worst thing that had happened to me.

Matt started picking again, and as I turned to do the same, I thought about the teenagers at Attawapiskat, about Rachel as a teen, and about my own teenage years. It hadn't been easy for me in the suburbs in the eighties, but I'd never felt like I did now. I'd wanted to get out, but out of where I was living, not out of my life. I tried to think about what it would have been like to grow up in an even smaller place so far from a city.

Matt moved to the yellow squash and there was a minute or two of silence before he picked up the conversation again. "So all of that was a very long answer, but still on the short side honestly. Did I answer your questions?"

"Yeah," I said, "Thank you for talking to me about it." But something about what he said was bothering me. "I was just thinking, though, if suicide's contagious and you're trying to get the teenagers and young adults to understand that and change course... how are you okay with the sanctuary being here and what people... do... here?"

Matt pursed his lips and blew air out through them slowly and audibly. He looked at me for a few seconds, and then looked down at the squash he was picking. When he spoke again, his voice was quieter and for the first time he seemed uncomfortable talking to me. "I'm not, entirely. But it's people at the end of their lives... your lives. It's different. Canadian and American settler societies don't provide a lot of options for people to die with dignity or spiritually come to terms with death. A lot of people don't have a community to hold them as they die, or any teachings to help them understand how to go through the process. A lot of people don't know how to find peace before they die, and it's really important to do that.

"So I respect what Catherine and Samu and the rest of the Society are doing in that regard, for people dealing with terminal illness who come from cultures that can't help them, or who are too disconnected from their own cultures to get the help they need. It's really different from kids and healthy young people trying to take their own lives out of desperation, on impulse. It's not the same thing, anyways."

Matt said this with such certainty and finality that I was sure Samu hadn't told him anything about my physical health. I wasn't about to tell him either, especially now. Talking to him about Rachel was one thing. Admitting to him, with the kind of work he did, that I just didn't feel able to go on, that I felt like there was nothing left worth doing . . . it would seem like nothing he'd just told me mattered. I contemplated whether my age made a difference. I wasn't, after all, a teenager. But I wasn't all that much older than Matt either. Maybe ten years. I couldn't think of any way to tell him. Instead, I asked, "Do other people in Attwawapiskat feel the way you do about the sanctuary?"

"I happen to be friends with Samu, so I'm privy to more information than other people, and I don't tend to ask Samu a lot of questions or talk to other people in town about it. People know the place is out here and that it helps people who are dying, and sometimes there's concern. But most people are focused on their own problems and don't have the emotional bandwidth to concentrate on what's going on out here."

He paused for a moment before concluding, uneasily. "They don't really feel like it's their problem how sick settlers with money choose to die. And the people on their way here don't tend to stay in town or have much contact with the community... and they don't tend to come back." He finished picking the vegetables in silence.

COUNTDOWN

A few days later, Catherine touched my arm as I entered the kitchen to make my drink, Ring padding behind me.

"I found a rescue in Winnipeg willing to take Ring. They have a spot opening up next week. We need to fly him next Wednesday."

I stared at her dumbly.

"It's a no-kill rescue," she continued. "They won't euthanize him. They'll find him a home."

"Will they keep him in a cage?" I asked.

"I don't know," Catherine said. "I didn't think to ask. It's not a shelter so I just assumed they'd keep him in someone's house, but I don't know."

I had no idea what day it was.

"When is next Wednesday?" My heart was palpitating.

"Six days from now," Catherine said. "Today's Thursday."

"Okay," I said, and Catherine looked relieved. But I did not feel relieved. I decided to ask.

"Is there any way to postpone it until I walk? I'd really like him to stay with me until then." She had told me to ask for what I wanted.

Catherine looked down, then met my eyes.

"I don't think so, Lee. They may not have a space then. They only have a space next week because one of their dogs is getting adopted, and they said they were moving Ring ahead of the dogs on their wait list due to the situation."

I nodded.

"Plus, really, how would that help him? I understand it might help you, but what about him? You really want him to get closer and closer to you and then lose you the way he lost Robert, and *then* go to the rescue? You've been so concerned about him this whole time."

"Also," she said after a few seconds of silence, "if his company is helping you so much, maybe that's something to think about. Why is it helping?"

"I feel connected to him," I answered and, thinking, added "and I'm taking care of him. It helps me to take care of him."

"But why does that help you?" she asked.

I stood trying to think about that, but my mind felt like a whirlpool, and anxiety was rising in my chest.

"You don't need to answer that now. You can think about it. I think you should think about it. If you're just feeling anxiety about him going, we can tap on that later."

I didn't want to tap on it. I wanted Ring to stay, and I wanted to feed him twice a day and take him outside and sleep with him on my bed until it was time for me to leave. But she was right—how would extra weeks of that help Ring if I was still going to leave him in the end? Was it fair to make him feel like I was now his caregiver and then pull that rug out from under him? Had I already done this?

Catherine turned to leave the kitchen, but immediately turned to face me again.

"Lee, when you think about it, I want you to also consider, at the same time, the feelings that made you—that still make you—want to walk. And where Ring fits into them. If it's too hard to think about on your own, wait and we'll do it when we tap. But I think it's important."

And with that, she left the room.

VIVIANA

After yoga and breathing in the lodge with Samu and Viviana, Ring and I were supposed to meet Catherine in the meditation hut. But I did not want to go. I asked Samu if I could take a break for an hour and build a fire. Ring loved the fire, as long as the door on the stove was closed, and I felt a drag on the momentum that usually kept me going from one activity to the next. I had grown to appreciate the way that moving through the day's activities blunted my thoughts and kept me more in my body than my head. But now I felt the need to think. I didn't tell Samu any of this, just waited for his answer.

Samu shrugged and smiled, said he'd let Catherine know, and walked his red stretch pants out of the room.

"Wanna join us?" I asked Viviana.

"Sure."

I got to work with the fire starter, impressed at how quickly I could now get a strong flame going. Ring stood back while I did this, but once I closed the door, he walked to a few feet in front of the stove, circled, and lay down with a contented groan. I moved back and sat on the nearest couch next to Viviana and we both stared at the flames.

"You know," she said after a while, "the stove is my favorite part of being here. I think it helps more than anything. If I do leave, I'm getting me a wood stove and I'm spending at least three hours a day staring at it." She sighed.

"How will you know?" I asked.

"Know what?"

"Whether to leave."

"Oh." She stared at the stove. "I don't know. I don't feel like I need to know that right now. I've been here about a month and a half. I'll see how I feel at three months, I guess. Catherine said I might be able to stay longer than that, depending on how full they are."

"They don't seem very full."

"No, but someone's coming. Did they tell you?"

I shifted in my seat. I'd been so consumed thinking about Ring leaving that I hadn't even wondered when the next guest would arrive.

"No," I said.

"An older woman named Gloria. Samu told me this morning. I think she's getting here in two days."

"Do you know anything about her?"

"He said she's in her late seventies, has a recurrence of breast cancer, and turned down chemo and radiation."

I looked at the flames. They expanded and contracted and expanded and contracted, reaching up and falling at the same time. It was mesmerizing, and something small within me let go while I watched. I almost forgot why I wanted to talk to Viviana. But then Ring sighed, and it prompted me to cut to the chase.

"They found a rescue in Winnipeg for Ring, for next week. They want to fly him there."

"How? In cargo?"

I started a bit. "I don't know. I didn't even think to ask. You think they'd put a dog in cargo?"

"Unless someone's flying with him, I think that's the only way they can do it. In a crate."

I frowned. "I don't know. I've never flown an animal."

"He'll be okay."

"He will?"

"He's doing a lot better than either of us. I think he'll be okay."

"You seem like you're doing well, to me," I said. "I don't know how, but you do."

Viviana closed her eyes. "Why do you say that?"

"You often seem upbeat, you help me, you help out around the sanctuary, you never look like you just want to lie on the floor like I feel."

"Well, you don't often lie on the floor, so I'm not sure you know what you look like from the outside either. But my issue is mostly anxiety, it being hard to feel safe. I don't have a problem getting up. I have a problem coming down. It's the opposite."

"I get anxiety sometimes too. Actually, I've had it more since I've been here, but to be fair, I was on Xanax before."

"Xanax, Klonopin, Valium, Buprenex, Lexapro, Wellbutrin, Prozac, Paxil…I've taken a lot of those drugs." She snorted. "Maybe all of them." She closed her eyes. "For a long time, I could barely sleep. Panic attacks whenever I was out somewhere public. Sometimes, I'd feel like I wasn't in my body. Unbearable."

"Are you off all the drugs now?"

"Almost. I had to get off the tranquilizers in order to come here, like you did, but you can't just stop antidepressants. It takes longer to taper them off, so I'm still working on it. But I feel calmer here than I have since…a long time…"

"I don't want Ring to go to a rescue," I said, guiltily aware I was veering away from Viviana's disclosures.

"Where do you want him to go?" she asked.

"That's the problem. I don't know. I want him to stay with me, but I don't want him to walk. I don't want him to keep losing people either, or be sent from place to place by himself. I just want to take care of him for now and not think about what happens later. I know that isn't fair. Catherine says I need to think about what it means and how it fits with me wanting to walk."

"Well, are you thinking about it?"

"I'm trying to right now. I do it better when I'm talking to you. If I try on my own, I just want to go to sleep."

"Well, why do you want Ring to stay with you?"

"I feel bad for him."

"That's it?"

"No. I want to take care of him. It helps me too."

"How does it help you?"

"I don't know. Maybe taking care of him makes me focus less on my own feelings of not wanting to be here, not wanting to be around. I feel like taking care of him is… something… some kind of…"

"Purpose?"

"Maybe. I don't know. I don't feel like I'm looking for a purpose."

"But you still feel it… with Ring."

"Maybe."

"Did it ever occur to you that taking care of him might fill in some of what you lost? You didn't only lose your daughter. There's a secondary kind of loss that comes with death—the loss of the relationship as well as the person. You took care of her, and now not only is she gone, but so is your job taking care of her."

I swallowed hard. "She was twenty-three. She wasn't even living in the same state as me. I hadn't been taking care of her for a while."

"You were, though, in some ways. You looked out for her, worried about her, right?"

I nodded but felt agitated and shifted in my seat. "Ring does not replace Rachel." I couldn't believe I actually needed to say that and wondered if I'd made a mistake trying to talk to Viviana.

"What? Of course not. That's not what I meant at all. I just meant part of your identity, who you were, was taking care of her, trying to help her live and be happy. And maybe a part of you needs to keep doing that in some way… for someone. And Ring's someone who's pretty easy to take care of."

"I don't know. I feel like that diminishes both Rachel and Ring in some way. Like it could be anyone. I don't think that's true."

"No, I didn't mean that at all. Look, why do you want to walk?"

"Same reason you do. I can't bear it."

"Can't bear what?"

"Feeling this way."

"What way?"

I looked at her blankly.

"I'm not trying to pick on you," Viviana said. "I'm just trying to think through it with you. That's what you wanted, isn't it?"

"This… empty, I guess. This much suffering."

"Lee, I want to ask you something. Don't get mad, because I've asked this of myself too, all the time, and I think it's important. What makes your suffering unique?"

"What do you mean?"

"I mean there are a lot of people in this world who have lost a child. There are a lot of women in this world who've gone through what I have too. A lot. Like, I don't know, probably millions. Over history, maybe billions. Suffering is everywhere. It's part of who we are, what we do. What makes yours so unique that it's impossible to withstand it when other people withstand it and keep going?"

This was not the first time I'd confronted this question.

"I've thought about that, you know. I've actually been thinking about it more since coming here, since I learned about the suicide crisis in Attawapiskat. Why so many young people there tried to take their own lives, how it gets to that point, why one kid and not another. I asked Matt about it when he was here. And the way he explained it, it's complicated. It's not just one thing. It has to do with intergenerational trauma and how much they feel part of their community, how much they're able to define their own experiences. But I'm not really sure how much that applies to me."

I paused, not sure how to communicate to Viviana everything I was thinking and feeling, not even sure how to articulate it to myself. "Before talking to Matt, I thought maybe the common denominator, for the teens and for me, was a lack of hope. That some people, for whatever reason, just lose the ability to hope for anything, to want anything. That's not what he said, but I still wonder if it's part of it. That they don't have what they feel like they need. It feels like it's gone and there's no way to get it back, or maybe it never existed in the first place, and so they try to kill themselves."

"Who, though? Are you talking about the whole community or a few people? Putting it that way sounds a little presumptuous, discriminatory even. Not everyone in Attawapiskat tries to kill themselves. Most people don't, even the people who have to live with both their own problems and a family member committing suicide. Most people there, like everywhere, go on. They have hard things in their lives and good things in their lives. We all do. Did everyone you met there look like they wanted to kill themselves? Does Matt seem like he wants to kill himself?"

"No, of course not. That's what I was trying to figure out. Why some people feel this way and other people in similar situations don't."

"So what do you think the difference is?"

"I don't know." I was feeling irritated, and looked directly at Viviana. It felt like we were talking in circles.

"Hey, you wanted to think it through with me. I'm just asking questions. Do you think I have the answer? I don't know the answer. I'm not trying to teach you anything. I'm literally just asking questions. If you want to stop talking about it, I'm late for working in the greenhouse."

"Sorry," I said, and we both looked at the fire. After a while, I spoke again, more quietly. "I guess it seems like part of it's about isolation. How much a person's able to feel connected to the people around them, responsible to a community, appreciative of being in a community. Or, instead, if they just feel alone." I sighed. "When Matt was talking to me about it, I kept thinking about Rachel, that she didn't have to deal with the kind of shit the kids in Attawapiskat have to deal with, but that maybe we still didn't give her enough community to handle what she did have to face.

"But I'm not sure that's true. Rachel didn't seem like she lacked community, or friends, or people who were important to her. She didn't … But maybe it's true of me. When she was here, I had her. Now she's gone and I don't know what I have. I let myself get isolated over the years. It was so gradual, it just seemed like a part of getting older. Your marriage wears out, your friends wear out, you focus more on your work. But it never happened to Susan. She stayed close to a lot of her friends, to some of her family. I'm not sure I was ever honest with myself about this, but I think I resented her for it, for being able to do that when I couldn't." I felt tears welling up.

Viviana was silent.

After a few moments, I spoke again. "Did you know suicide's contagious?"

"What?"

"Matt told me that. That the single biggest risk for someone killing themselves is knowing someone else who did."

Viviana raised her eyebrows. She looked thoughtful. "That makes sense with a lot of what I've seen with the veterans I know."

"Does it make you worry about what you're doing here? That it could affect anyone else?"

"I think I always knew that what I do here would affect other people. I have three sisters. It's part of why I'm not committed to walking.… What about you?"

"I've been thinking more about Susan. I'm worried about what it will do to her. I also wonder if it's part of the reason I'm here. I don't think Rachel took her own life. I really don't, but if I'm honest with myself, I don't really know. It's unbearable to think she could have done it on purpose."

After a few moments of quiet, I realized I'd never really answered Viviana's question. Maybe I hadn't wanted to answer it. But I tried now. "I guess maybe my suffering isn't unique. Maybe, besides the isolation, I'm just weaker than other people."

"Really? You think you're weak?"

"I know I'm weak. I can't bear to be alive. I also can't seem to do myself in. I'm afraid of both."

"Lee. Seriously. You called this place you saw in a guidebook, left everything and everyone you knew, traveled for days on planes and trains up to where polar bears live, then came here, where you spend your days getting into bathtubs full of ice water and snowshoeing for miles and talking to people who are dying or so messed up they're ready to die. While in this state, you take on caring for someone else's dog and riding in a snowmobile with a dead body. But you think you're weak?"

I focused on the flames for a while and then turned and looked at Viviana's face. She really did look flabbergasted. She continued.

"You know, with everything I think about myself and every problem I've had surviving what happened to me, I never once thought I was weak. Maybe it's because of my time in the army. I got through basic training. I saw combat. Soldiers depended on me. I know I can best just about anybody in a fair fight. There's a lot of bullshit in the army about weakness. Even though I lived with that bullshit for years, I do not feel weak. And you're not weak either. That is not what's going on."

"Then what is going on? You just asked me what makes my suffering unique. What makes your suffering unique. Other people go on—you said it yourself. It can't just be isolation. Some people are alone and still survive. If it's not weakness, what is it? Why can other people go on and we can't?"

Now she was staring at the fire.

"I don't know, but I actually think we are going on. So far, we're both going on. We're here having this conversation. We're here growing and cooking our own food, taking ice baths, working our bodies, training our minds. I think we're both going on."

"But the goal here is to not go on. We're both here because of that option."

"Yeah, well, I don't think keeping my options open and having an escape hatch makes me weak. I don't think spies holding onto cyanide as a way to get out of being tortured are weak. I don't think my friends with PTSD who killed themselves were weak. Are you saying the teens in Attawapiskat who took their own lives were weak? Would you say that to Matt about the kids he's trying to help?

"We've all got our limits. I don't know what makes one person's limits different than another's. I'm staring some of my limits in the face here every day and I'm still not sure where they are, or if they move. And I also don't think that contemplating the end of my life, or thinking about surrendering my life, is the same as doing it. And I haven't done it yet and I don't know that I ever will. I don't think looking all the options in the face is a sign of weakness. Especially the way we're doing it."

I leaned back and closed my eyes. "And what about Ring's options? How do I consider the options for someone else? I feel like it's weak of me to not just adopt him and take him home. And maybe I would, if I had somewhere that still felt like home. I don't even know where home would be. Home is a dark hole right now. Who knows what Ring's limits are. No one's asking him. We might be crashing through every one of them by sending him in cargo on some plane to Winnipeg, to strangers who might put him in a cage and then, if he's lucky, send him home with other strangers after who knows how long. What if that's beyond his limit? What happens to dogs pushed past their limits?"

Viviana looked at me skeptically. This irritated me at first, like she wasn't taking what I said seriously. But then I realized why she was looking at me that way. "Do you think I'm exaggerating how hard this would be for Ring? You think this is more about me than Ring, don't you? That's obviously what Catherine thinks. Is she right? Is this about me not wanting to let Ring go?"

"I don't know. But maybe now you have some idea why Robert decided to take him with him. Robert didn't have the choice to keep going. He was going to die wherever he was, and he was going to leave Ring to just the kind of situation you're worried about. Maybe what he did was about him and not Ring. You certainly seemed to think so. Or maybe he knew sending Ring to a shelter was past Ring's limit. I don't pretend to know the answer to that, though I suspect Ring would adjust. But maybe you can have a little more sympathy for Robert now."

"I have to admit," I said quietly, "that has occurred to me. I've only known Ring since I've been here. Robert had him for nine years. I still don't think what he tried to do was okay. But I don't know what the answer is."

GLORIA

Gloria arrived two days later, a little after sunset. Short and thickly built with pale pinkish skin and wispy short gray hair, she entered the lodge from the snow with a smile on her face.

"Well," she said, looking around at me and Viviana and the wood stove, "I've made it." She took off her outer layers and, without waiting for an invitation, sat down on the chair nearest the fire. Catherine left for the kitchen for motherwort and sage tea, apparently her welcome to every new guest.

Gloria reached into the pocket of her parka lying on the chair next to her, pulled out a thin metal case, and put on a pair of wire-rimmed glasses.

"Couldn't wear them with the goggles," she announced, to no one in particular or perhaps to me and Viviana. "That ride was bracing. Haven't felt so good in ages."

She smiled again and turned to me and then Viviana in turn. "I'm Gloria."

Viviana and I introduced ourselves. After that, there was silence for a while, other than Gloria's repeated sighing as she stared at the flames. Eventually, she spoke again.

"Where are you girls from?"

I was slightly taken aback, as no one had referred to me as a girl in a very long time. I looked at Viviana, her muscles and her cropped hair, and she smiled at me in amusement.

"I'm from Atlanta," Viviana offered and, when I said nothing, added "and Lee's from Madison, Wisconsin. We're both from the U.S. And you? Where did you come from today?"

"Oh, I'm a local girl compared to the two of you," Gloria responded cheerfully. "I'm from Churchill. I mean, not originally. Originally I'm from Winnipeg, but I've been living in Churchill for over three decades now." She smiled. "Oh, I guess I should say I *was* living there. Don't live there anymore, do I?" Her smile seemed so genuine it looked almost stupid.

Viviana looked annoyed. At first, I thought that she, like me, was irritated by Gloria's cheerfulness, but it suddenly dawned on me that she was annoyed at me for my reticence.

"Well," Viviana said, "welcome to the sanctuary. I hope you get a lot out of being here, and we're glad you came. What did you do in Churchill?"

"I ran a little hotel," she answered. "That's maybe a *glori*fied thing to call it." She looked at us slyly, which confused me, until I realized she was trying to make a pun. This amazed me. This small cheerful woman had just left everything she knew to take her final refuge in a place where she'd likely die, and here she was, hoping we'd noticed her pun. She continued, "It's really more like a bed and breakfast. There's only four guestrooms, but we called it a hotel."

"That's great," Viviana said. "Who's we?"

"Oh, my husband Don and me. But he's dead almost ten years now. I've been running it myself. Or I was til my last round of treatment last year. It's been closed since then. My sister came to stay with me. It was just the two of us these last eight months or so."

"It's not the one with the glass domes on the roof, is it?" I asked. Viviana's amusement grew.

"Oh no," said Gloria, "nothing that fancy. That place is big, has at least twenty rooms. Hotel Gloria's only four rooms. Was only four rooms."

"Is that really the name of it?" I asked.

"Oh yes, that's what we named it. Hotel Gloria. Really wonderful, it was."

"Is someone taking over running it?" I asked.

"My sister's still there for now, but she's closing up the building until she can sell it. I'm leaving it to her, but she doesn't want to run a hotel. She's older than I am. She's seventy-eight, and she's got family to get back to in Winnipeg. So Hotel Gloria is *closing up shop*, just like Gloria herself!" She was smiling broadly at us.

Catherine walked in with the tea. "Gloria," she said. "You relax here a while and the rest of us will make dinner." She nodded to us, and we got up and walked with her toward the kitchen.

As I started walking, Ring stretched and yawned and peeled off to join Gloria by the fire. "That's Ring," I said. "He likes the stove. And anyone who'll pet him."

LIGHTS

"That doesn't make you uncomfortable?" I asked Viviana as we sat wrapped up on the observation deck waiting for the lights.

"What, that she's friendly?"

"No, that she's cheerful. She's dying of breast cancer and just seems delighted by everything."

Viviana was silent for a long time, sighing and looking up at the sky. In the darkness, she seemed like a padded lump of material, her hooded head tilting back. Eventually she spoke.

"Every single person dies. Every single one. There's seven billion human beings on the planet right now who are going to die, and there must be billions who already have. Add in all the other animals and the bugs and the bacteria, and this whole place is basically one giant stampede toward death. So if someone's able to accept that cheerfully, I say more power to her. I certainly think it's more honorable than what we're doing."

Now I was silent for a bit, considering that. "You think what we're doing isn't honorable?"

"I spent years working every day to survive in Iraq. I know you don't understand this, but I'm still working to survive. Every day, I'm still doing it. I know that's not how you view what you're doing, but it's what I'm doing here day to day. And I'm maybe getting better at it. I think that's honorable. I don't really see anything honorable, though, in deciding nothing here is worth the work. I know you think I came here to die, but I came here to try to live, even if for a short time. We're all just trying to live for a short time. And Gloria has a short time, and she's happy to spend it here and to learn how to live it, how to pass through the way the Society teaches. How can you hold that against her, that she's okay with that?"

"I don't know. I guess it doesn't seem real to me … like how can anyone actually live like that?"

"Lee, are you able to live the way you are? You think you're a model for how to do this?"

As I contemplated that, Ring wiggled against my leg under the blanket, pressing his nose into my knee.

Viviana spoke again. "Did it occur to you that maybe she's happy it's almost over? Her husband died ten years ago. She's in her mid-seventies. She's been living in one of the coldest places on earth, taking care of other people."

"I'm sorry. I didn't mean to upset you."

We were both quiet, waiting for the lights. Only Ring made noise—little snuffling sounds as he nosed around for a better position and crinkled the foil blanket.

But the lights didn't come.

MORNING

Ring and I were just finishing up in the kitchen when Catherine motioned to me to come over. She had been showing Gloria how to make her green drinks. Gloria's tired smile never left her face as she nodded at leaves of spinach and handfuls of frozen blueberries. I had made my drink quickly and quietly and was trying to leave for my morning work in the greenhouse.

"Lee, I want you to take Gloria with you to the greenhouse and show her what to do." Catherine watched my face as I listened to her. I was truly startled by this request.

"What do you mean?" I asked.

"I mean, just take her in, show her what I showed you the first day about the soil, give her a tour of the greenhouse, and let her help you with your work. I have other things I need to do, and you're capable of showing her everything."

I could not think of anything I would less like to do with my morning. But I found myself nodding, since I had no good reason to refuse Catherine's request. I looked over at Gloria, and she was beaming at me. I absentmindedly reached down and patted Ring's side.

As we made our way out the kitchen door into the walkway, Gloria stopped and loudly inhaled. "I know it's dark, but I can already tell it's going to be a glorious day. Can't you?" she asked, looking at me from under the rim of her parka hood.

I wasn't sure what she meant and told her so.

"Sunny. I can tell it's going to be really sunny today, really beautiful. Can't you feel that? I've been able to tell for years now, waking up early and getting the hotel ready for the guests while they slept. It's something about the color of the dark, and the particular sounds. The way there's almost a little glow at the horizon even though I know the sun won't rise for hours. Can you see it?"

I looked but I honestly couldn't. I could see vague outlines that I knew were the huts and the platform, and I could see a few stars, but there was some cloud cover, too, so I couldn't understand the prediction of sun. I bounced up and down a little trying to stay warm while we stood on the walkway. Ring pressed himself against my legs.

Eventually, Gloria started walking again, and we entered the greenhouse.

As I lowered my parka hood, the warmth and moisture hitting the skin on my face was a welcome and familiar feeling. I breathed in through my nose and smelled the mustiness of the dirt. Glancing at the white board, I saw a longer list of tasks than usual.

"Catherine's never asked me to teach anything before," I said to Gloria apologetically. "I guess I'll start with what Catherine first showed me—the soil and how to feel it with your fingers. And then I'll show you around and the basics of what we do here, and then we can get started."

"I feel like we've already gotten started," said Gloria pleasantly, as she took off her parka and gloves. She looked at me expectantly and, of course, she was smiling.

As I talked to her about the microbes in the soil and their effects on the brain, and we squatted with our fingers in the loose soil in the scallion bed, Gloria nodded and theatrically inhaled and exhaled.

After a few minutes, we stood and I showed her around the greenhouse: the heating and irrigation systems, the compost bin, the weeding and aerating tools, the buckets for picking. I then divided up tasks for us to accomplish separately, looking forward to hearing only my own hands working and Ring's breathing next to me.

But Gloria wanted to talk, and so she did.

From two beds over, examining and picking green beans, she called to me loudly. "You know, I don't think I've ever felt as free as I do right now! It's almost intoxicating."

I did not know how to respond to this. I didn't even know how to comprehend it. I just kept picking kale. But she continued.

"My whole life, I did what was expected of me. I mean, no one expected me to marry a guy from Churchill and run a hotel for people looking to see polar bears, but you know what I mean. I had work, I did it every day, I supported myself, I talked to people, I washed sheets, I cooked. I never really stopped for much, even when Don died. At first, I felt like I couldn't go on, but of course I did. You do. Everyone does. We had guests at the time and I made the beds as always, cooked breakfast. It kept me going, you know? I kept going. Now I get to stop. It's very exciting."

"Stopping is exciting?" I asked, incredulous. It really did sound like she was excited to come die. I suppose I had felt that to some extent, but not like this. Just enough to get myself here, but barely.

"I've always known I'm going to die, of course, but now I feel like I can really live, too. Realizing how little time I have left, or might have left—it's freeing. I feel free. Like I can do anything. Like everything looks bigger and brighter. Things smell stronger—the dirt, the tea, the fire. I'm doing something I want to do, something I've thought about for a long time. Just stopping the whole hamster wheel and coming here, with no expectations.

"I mean, I haven't worked in over eight months. It's not that. But even the treatments—they were what was expected. I can't say I really wanted to do them, and I was so sick from them. I know I'll be sick again, but for now I feel pretty good, and I'm here, and it's exciting. I feel more like me than I have in a long time. You know… when you're around family, even if you love them like I love my sister, it's hard to really be yourself because they have such a strong expectation of who you are and what you should be like.

"When you leave, it's freeing. I mean, it's sad too—I'll miss my sister. But here I am. I thought Churchill was remote, but look where we are. What a way to end the journey! Just marvelous! I feel so lucky! They wanted me to go to hospice. No thank you. I feel too good for hospice. I've had my eye on this place for a while and now I'm finally here…"

She went on, talking about the garden she had at the hotel in summer, flowers mostly, how different vegetable gardening is, how she'd never been a vegetarian because it's not something her family would ever have understood, but she's excited to try it. How she was really looking forward to getting out on snowshoes as she hadn't done that in years but had watched her guests enjoying it. After twenty minutes of listening to her chatter, I wanted to lie down on the dirt floor and close my eyes. But I moved on to the broccoli bed.

"Viviana told me you have breast cancer too," Gloria said, and I almost dropped the knife I was using to cut the stalks.

"No, I don't. I mean, I did. I had a mastectomy, but I've been in remission a long time. I don't think I have it now."

Gloria stopped picking and stood up, wiping her face with the back of her arm.

"You're in remission?" she asked, surprised.

"Yes. At least I think so. I haven't had a scan in a while."

"So what do you have now?" she asked, earnestly.

No one had asked me this since I'd arrived. Catherine and Samu had told Robert and Viviana my situation before I got here, and I'd assumed they'd tell Gloria as well. I was silent, trying to think of what to say.

"My daughter died." I said softly.

Gloria's face fell. "Oh, I'm so sorry. So sorry. My daughter died too."

I stopped what I was doing and stood up, looking at her. "Your daughter died too?"

"Yes. At birth. She died at birth. I still think of her every day. I talk to her. Denise. Her name's Denise. I talk to her all the time. I'm looking forward to seeing her again."

I didn't know what to say. Gloria was in her mid-seventies. Her daughter must have died at least thirty or forty years ago.

While I was thinking this, she asked, "How old was your daughter?"

"Twenty-three." I heard myself respond as if from somewhere far away.

"How amazing. Twenty-three years. I can't tell you what I would give to have had twenty-three years with Denise. To see her grow up. Heaven—it would have been heaven."

"She was just getting started," I said, uncomfortable.

"Of course she was. I'm sorry. I just meant how wonderful you had that time with her. We all have different amounts of time. I can't quite believe I made it to seventy-six. Don didn't make it past sixty-eight. Denise's whole life was inside of me—she didn't make it to one day old. At least she had that. At least I got to see her and hold her." Gloria wiped a tear away from her right eye with the back of her wrist. "Seems like yesterday. It was forty-two years ago. She'd be forty-two now." She smiled again. "How long ago did you lose your daughter?"

I realized, for the first time, that I'd lost track of how long I'd been at the sanctuary, that I wasn't sure how much time had passed since I'd arrived. "About eleven months ago," I said flatly. Gloria looked surprised.

"And you were already sick? Or did you get sick after?"

"I'm… not physically sick. I'm just… struggling… finishing up…"

"Oh. You're depressed." Gloria said, matter-of-factly, looking sorry.

It was true. Clearly it was true. It just sounded much too simple, like a state of mind, or an illness, or an experience. When what it was, really, was the narrowing of my life to a point, with no room for movement except deeper into the narrow place I was pushing toward. But I didn't say anything.

"Oh my goodness. You're so young. What a terrible thing." Gloria stood there, looking speechless for once. But she wasn't. She continued.

"I guess I always thought it would have been easier if Denise had lived into childhood, that every year she was alive would have made it better, easier to handle her death. She had so little chance, and I had so little time to do anything for her. I always wanted to do things for her. I gave her a funeral. I made her a memorial in my garden. I donated money to funds for childhood diseases. But I really just wanted to hold her, to feed her, to see her learn to crawl and walk. And no one understood at the time, you know, a stillbirth.

People didn't think of her as a real child, as my daughter, just as something that happened. Would you believe one of my friends compared it to losing her belongings when her house flooded? Really, that's what she compared it to, and she was trying to be understanding. I never spoke to her again. I kind of regret that—she didn't know what to say—but it felt like she was erasing my daughter's life. My daughter wasn't furniture."

Dumbfounded, I bent over and started cutting stalks again.

"Oh, Gloria, you are always talking too much!" she said, and bent back to work in her own bed. "I'm sorry about that. And I'm so sorry about your daughter. What was her name?"

"Rachel," I said, surprised her name came out in one piece, calmly, as if she were still alive.

"Well, I suspect Rachel was lucky to have you too. I'm very sorry you lost her. Did you go to a support group? I went to a small support group at the hospital back when it happened. It was so helpful. No one else really understood what we were going through. It was terrible for Don too. After that, we moved back to Churchill—well, back for him—and bought the hotel. Needed to be somewhere new, and do something different. Well, new to me. Don had grown up there. But being with strangers, having a routine, and seeing all these excited young tourists arriving each week to see the polar bears and go kayaking and things, it really helped. Is that why you're here?"

I wasn't sure and told her so. Maybe yes to the routine, no to the kayaking. "I guess I just wanted a quiet place, with people dealing with hard things, and a way out that didn't feel violent. And I didn't want anyone I knew to find me. I didn't want to do that to anyone."

"Someone always finds you, dear. There's really no way to do this without someone finding you. They'll find you here too."

"But they're okay with it. It won't ruin their lives. I didn't want to ruin anyone's life."

"What about Rachel's father?" Gloria asked.

I stood again and looked at her dumbly. Living in Madison for decades had made me unused to this.

"Rachel had another mother—my wife Susan. We've split up." I fought back a lump in my throat.

"Oh, it just keeps getting worse. I'm so sorry." Gloria said. "So you're a lesbian then?" She smiled sweetly and looked almost proud of herself.

"No, actually I'm non-binary." We looked at each other blankly.

"I'm sorry?" Gloria asked.

"I'm non-binary. I'm not male or female. When I was younger, I did identify as lesbian, but it never felt right and I eventually realized I'm non-binary."

"But you're physically a woman?" she asked.

"No, I don't think so. I don't feel like it and at this point I have one breast and no ovaries. If you're asking what my genitals look like, I don't normally discuss that with strangers. Do you?"

Gloria inhaled sharply, loudly enough for me to hear. I immediately regretted talking to her in that way. She was a seventy-six-year-old woman from a tiny town in the snow where people arrived on the slowest train on earth to see polar bears. It shouldn't have been shocking that she wasn't up to speed on gender identities.

"I'm sorry, Gloria," I said. "I realize you weren't trying to offend me, and honestly, I'm beyond caring all that much. That answer was just reflexive. Please forgive me."

"Oh no, I'm sorry. I obviously did offend you and I didn't mean to. I admit I'm a little confused, but I'm happy to learn about these things. You may think a dying seventy-six-year-old can't learn new things, but I'm here to do exactly that, and I'm happy to. I'm glad to know you're non-binary. That's wonderful. It's wonderful there are so many ways for us to be ourselves. I'm looking forward to finding out more of them."

Thinking the conversation was over, I moved to return the tools to their places and start watering.

"And Ring?" Gloria asked as she followed me to the hose. "How long have you had him? He's darling."

"Just since I've been here. He was here before me, with a man who already walked. Robert." I felt tears well up, surprising me.

"Oh, he lives here? I thought he was your dog."

"He… doesn't live here. He's leaving. They're sending him to a rescue in a few days." The ache returned in my chest, which made me realize, with surprise, that it had been gone for some unknown length of time.

"Oh, that's a shame. He seems so attached to you. I've always loved dogs. Always had at least one dog almost my whole life. My last dog, Sadie, died two years after Don, and I never got another. I was done with death, so I didn't adopt again. I didn't want to lose another dog. Of course, as it turns out, you're never really done with death." Gloria smiled brightly.

SITTING

As I entered the meditation hut with Ring later that morning, Catherine greeted me with a nod and smile and said, "We're going to do something different today. I think you need to sit with yourself."

Confused, I looked at her with slightly squinted eyes as I sat down on a cushion. "Isn't that what I normally do in here?" I asked. Ring was turning in little circles, the way he did just before lying down.

"You're usually meditating on your breath. Yes, in some way, that's sitting with yourself, but it's not what I mean for today. Today, I want you to sit with your emotions, to feel them in your body without trying to get rid of them or get away from them." She looked at me expectantly.

I was silent.

"Lee, I think you're still afraid of feeling what you're feeling. You've been doing a lot of good work here and I see a difference, but there's still this energy coming from you. An energy of trying to shut out your emotions. Because they scare you."

"They do scare me."

"I know they do, but trying to get away from them doesn't make them go away. It makes them stronger. They're eating you alive."

"Well, I figure they eat me alive and then I'm done." I shifted on the cushion.

"No, you're done when you let them move through you. We've done this together with tapping, and with the myofascial release, but you need to do more of it, and I think you're ready to do it more directly. Whether you know it or not, this is what you came here for. You need to face this, to feel the emotions and get to the other side of them, and then see what's left after. Otherwise, you're just living like a zombie and making decisions out of fear."

She paused, looking at me intently like she was trying to make sure I was listening before she continued. "In the end, everything comes down to love or fear. You have a lot of love in you... I know you do. But you're so afraid of facing what's inside you that you're controlled by your fear. You can't make a decision to walk that way. You can't walk out of fear."

"What does it mean to *sit with it*? I need to sit and think of Rachel? I think about Rachel constantly."

"It's not thinking. It's feeling. They're not the same thing. You've convinced yourself they're the same thing, but they're not. Feeling happens in your body. It's the energy that's released when we tap. You've been letting little bits of it come out that way, and I've seen the relief, but you've been poking holes in the dam. It's time for a sledgehammer."

I rubbed my face with my hands, trying to take this in, my chest tightening. Whatever this was, I didn't want it.

"Close your eyes and take a deep breath. Settle into your body like you're going to meditate, only don't focus on your breath. You can be aware of it, but that's not where you're going. I just want you to feel your body. You don't need to think about anything at all. In fact, whenever you start thinking, I want you to just sink into your body and feel it. Your emotions are in your body. They're not in your head. That's right, let your breath be slow and calm. But tell me: What does your body feel like right now?"

"My legs are tired and sore," I offered. I had snowshoed over a mile and a half the day before and, this morning in the greenhouse, squatted more than usual. Gloria's presence had made resting breaks seem less palatable.

"Okay, good. Your legs are tired and sore. Where in your legs? Be more specific about what it feels like."

"My quads and my calves. They feel heavy and slightly painful. Sore, like the muscles are a little bruised."

"How much does it hurt?"

"I don't know. Enough for me to notice it, I guess, but not excruciating. It's not a bad soreness."

"Okay, good. Now focus on what your stomach, your chest, and your head feel like. Take your time. Can you locate anything that feels like an emotion? Like fear, sadness, anger, happiness, love?"

I sank deeper into my body. I had been less aware of the aching in my chest lately, at least during activities. I was more aware of it in bed at night cuddling Ring and waiting for sleep.

"My chest."

"What does it feel like?"

"Ache."

"Ache like your legs?"

"No, different than my legs."

"What does it feel like?"

I opened my eyes.

"Don't open your eyes. Just sit and feel it until you have an answer. There's no rush."

I felt it. It was like a volcano pushing against my ribcage.

"It's more uncomfortable. It feels like pressure. Pain also. A deep strong ache that hurts, but it's mostly a feeling of pressure, like there's something pressing against my sternum from the inside, like some expanding ball, or a volcano, but it's not hot and it's not coming out, just pushing and pushing."

"Lee, that's really good. If we were tapping, we'd tap on those words, but what I want you to do right now is just sit and feel that. Really feel it. Allow it to be."

"It's uncomfortable. I don't want to focus on it."

"So be uncomfortable. Surely coming here, you expected on some level to be uncomfortable. Your body is pushing you—your spirit is pushing you—to accept this feeling. Running from it doesn't relieve it. It just makes it chase you. Try to sit with it. It will get better, but only on the other side.... I want you to feel the texture, the shape of it. What shape is it?"

"A hollow cylinder."

"What color is it?"

"Ice blue."

"What texture is it?"

"Smooth, with little cracks."

"Look into the hollow blue cylinder with the cracks, Lee. There's an emotion inside it. What's the emotion?"

"Emotion?"

"Emotion."

"Anxiety?"

"Anxiety isn't actually an emotion. It's a reaction. It's the discomfort we feel from not accepting our emotions, from trying to avoid feeling them. Fear is an emotion. Sadness is an emotion. Anxiety is a stress state."

"Emptiness. Sadness...."

"Good."

"Fear. An afraid kind of sadness, if that makes sense."

"It does," Catherine said reassuringly. "Okay, I want you to focus your attention on that feeling—the aching and pressure in your chest. Give it your attention like you would pay attention to your breath in meditation. Every once in a while, ask it what it needs."

"Ask *what* what it needs?" I opened my eyes again briefly, then closed them.

"Ask the aching what it needs. It may answer; it may not. It may just need you to accept it and pay attention to it. It may need something else. It may take a long time for it to tell you. Just be open to it. Tell it you're not running from it anymore, that you're ready to listen."

I sat, feeling the ache, wondering how many minutes this part of the exercise would go on for.

"Okay," Catherine offered, audibly rising to her feet. "I want you to do this for an hour."

"*What?*" I objected, opening my eyes again and leaving them open.

"I'll come check on you periodically," Catherine said softly. "And when I do, I don't want you to open your eyes or do anything to greet me. I'll bring a bell with me and I'll ring it, and that will be a reminder to you that whatever you're doing or thinking about, you should come back to your body, find where the ache is, and listen to it. If the ache moves or changes into something else, follow it and pay attention to it. You may be surprised what it turns into. I'm not going to come in at regular intervals. At first, I'll come in after a short while, and then I'll return after longer but irregular intervals. Don't try to anticipate it."

"For an hour?" My eyes were closed again.

"For an hour." With that, Catherine left the hut.

In the silence that followed, I could hear Ring breathing near the wall in front of me.

I focused on the lump in my chest swelling and writhing. I saw it as a blue and black mass with tentacles, gripping onto my rib cage from the inside and constricting my heart. I breathed into it, looked at it, asked it what it wanted. I tried to listen. But all I could hear was Ring breathing against the wall.

Ring. What to do about Ring? In a few days, he'd be put in a crate and sent somewhere on a plane. He knew nothing of this. Was just lying by the wall breathing.

Around and around I went, back to the tentacled mass in my chest, trying to focus on it seething and lashing, waiting for it to unfurl, then slipping away in my mind to Ring's breathing and how I could hear his chest moving up and down in the silence. I felt like I needed to lie down, and sank back onto the floor without opening my eyes.

And then I heard it—the bell, the ringing. It startled me back to my own senses, my shoulders against the rug, my own chest moving up and down, the lump inside. I tried to focus my attention on it, to do as Catherine asked. But instead of unfurling and releasing, it got bigger and grabbed onto me more furiously, emitting some kind of ink that filled the cavity in my chest with cold fluid like ice water. I saw it black and murky, paralyzing everything but my heart, which beat faster and faster until it was pounding so hard that I gasped and called out.

I opened my eyes. I could not do this for an hour—would not do this for an hour. I understood it was supposed to help, but I had to get up, had to leave the hut. Now.

I called Ring and we walked quickly out into the courtyard, where I felt the sting of the cold on my face. I hadn't put my hat on or pulled up my hood, and the bare skin exposed to the air burned. The air was blowing against me—the wind. I stood there and closed my eyes and inhaled the cold air, feeling the pain in my lungs, feeling the tentacled thing in my chest shrink back and freeze.

Maybe I needed to go back into the hut and concentrate on it. But I felt like I needed to run, and that's what I did. I ran, Ring close behind me, over to the covered walkway, in through the kitchen, and down the hall to the main room.

GLORIA'S HOTEL

Gloria was sitting on a chair she'd pulled very close to the fire, which was burning even though it was morning. It was still dark outside, and the flames were bright. I stopped short when I saw her, and Ring bumped into the back of my legs so that they started to buckle. I reached down with my hand and steadied myself on his back.

"Whoa" slipped out of my mouth. Ring licked my hand, then walked over to Gloria and pressed himself against her knees. She smiled and reached to pet him.

"Well, hello, you." Gloria tilted her head to the side, running her hand over Ring's back. "I do miss having a dog around. I'm so glad you're here." Then she looked up at me. "Too bad he's leaving."

I swallowed but did not answer.

"Sit down, Lee. I'm recovering."

"From what?" I asked, sitting on the couch slightly behind and to the right of her.

"From five minutes of yoga," Gloria said with a chuckle. "Never thought I'd start yoga on my deathbed." She smiled wide. I could not get used to her smile. "Don't sit behind me like that. Pull up a chair. The fire's delicious."

I hesitated but without thinking found myself pulling a chair closer to the stove so that I was just a few feet from Gloria. Ring had lain down by her feet.

"You don't really want to send this dog to that shelter, do you? He's such a nice dog. You should keep him."

"It's not my choice," I said. "Catherine said he can't stay."

"Can't you take him with you when you leave?" asked Gloria.

"I wasn't planning on leaving," I responded. "I'm planning to stay until I walk."

Gloria sighed, staring at the fire. We were both silent a few minutes. My eyes started to feel heavy from the warmth.

"You're a young girl."

"I'm neither young nor a girl," I said, feeling irritated.

"Okay." She was silent again.

"You know," she said, "it was a strange feeling leaving the hotel for the last time. I thought it would be really hard, after so many years. But it was a relief. It was a relief because I'd finished, you know? I was finished with it. It was what I did after Denise died, what I created to find a way to live after Denise, and I did that. And now I don't need to anymore."

I didn't say anything.

"But it was still strange. Because even though I didn't need to be there, it seemed like someone did. Like the place was waiting for something. For someone."

"Your sister?" I asked.

"My sister is almost eighty years old. The hotel is not waiting for my sister. My sister will have enough trouble selling it." Gloria sighed again. Ring sighed in response. I almost sighed myself; the warmth of the fire was getting to me.

"Why don't you take it for a while?" Gloria asked quietly.

"Take what?"

"The hotel."

"What?"

"You could take a break from here for a while. I don't think this place is going anywhere. Take Ring there. It's a good place for a dog. You can take over my watch, just for a while. I created it to learn how to live after my daughter died. You can step into it, see if you can find a way to live without your daughter. Give that dog a home. You can always come back here later. You could continue what you're doing here, make the hotel a place for people who want to do this kind of thing without the walk, make it some kind of wellness adventure package. I've been thinking about it all morning."

She looked serious.

"I have no interest in running a hotel." I thought I was beyond being astonished by anything.

"To be honest, I didn't have any interest in running a hotel either. It was just a place to be, and I met a lot of people."

"I don't want to meet a lot of people." In fact, I was wishing I hadn't met Gloria.

"It's cozy. You could put in a sauna there, and there's a big bathtub you could use for ice baths. You could build a little greenhouse. Offer yoga and meditation. Just to a few people at a time. Remember, there's only four rooms. But what a great place for a dog."

Who was this woman? Why did she want to give me her hotel?

"Maybe you're having a harder time letting go of the hotel than you thought," I offered.

"No. I've let go of the hotel. I don't like seeing you let go of the dog, or the memory of your daughter. Or your life."

"I'm *not* letting go of the memory of my daughter!" I felt angry now.

"No, not while you're alive, but what happens to it after you walk out into the snow? You gave her a few months of grieving, and then that's it?" Gloria smiled weakly. "I gave my daughter the rest of my life. Every person I took care of in that hotel was for my daughter. I couldn't take care of her, so I took care of them. And my dogs. Until it was over."

I got up to leave.

"I'm sorry, Lee, I just can't see you walking out into the snow when your cancer is in remission."

"It has nothing to do with my cancer." I was exasperated.

"Exactly," she said. "So why not do something else for a while? You like snowshoeing? You can snowshoe out the door of the hotel every day."

"Gloria, do I look like someone who can cook breakfast and turn down beds for tourists? Do I look like someone who wants to do that?"

"No. You look like someone who needs a place to grieve your daughter and go snowshoeing and take care of this dog. And take saunas and ice baths. The other people are extra."

"Why don't you ask Viviana?" I said. "Why me?"

"I will," she said. "But I feel bad for the dog."

"I feel bad for the dog too," I said, and left him lying by her feet as I started to walk out toward my room. Turning around, I added, with more anger than I intended, "But this isn't some kind of riddle for you to fix. You can't just fix things because you don't like the way they are. The world doesn't work that way. I wouldn't suddenly be okay by doing what you did, just because you were, just because you want me to be." I started walking again, a surge of something hot rising in my chest.

"I didn't say I was okay!" Gloria called after me. "I said it helped me. And I didn't say you'd be okay. You don't have to be okay. You just need to give this dog a home. You can always commit suicide later. I can't but you can. I've left the life that helped me, that helped me live without my daughter. Why don't you take it for a while?"

VIVIANA

"I left the hut after maybe twenty minutes. I couldn't do it."

Viviana was wrapped in a foil blanket, her knees hunched against her chest, looking at me without expression.

"I don't know what that means," I continued. "Does it mean I have to stay here until I can focus on my feelings for an hour? Is that a requirement?"

Viviana considered, then smiled a little. "Nah. I think you need to be able to go a lot longer than an hour."

"That's not funny."

"Did I say it was funny?" She raised her left eyebrow and pursed her lips.

Ring got up and circled under the blanket, then lay back down.

"Viviana, I had the weirdest experience with Gloria in the lodge this morning." I recounted the conversation to her and, while I spoke, she put her head on her folded arms, which were on her knees. "Isn't that bizarre?"

Viviana nodded slowly and started rocking back and forth like she did.

"Yes," she said. "It's bizarre."

The lights didn't seem to be coming. I shifted, getting cold even under the blanket with Ring.

"It's bizarre," she repeated. "But it also kinda makes sense."

"That she'd say that?"

"Yeah, that she'd say that…. But also doing it kinda makes sense."

"How can you say that? I have no desire to run a hotel. If you think it makes sense, why don't you do it?"

"She didn't ask me."

"I'm sure she would ask you. She told me she asked me because she feels bad for Ring."

"Well, you and Gloria have that in common. You both feel bad for Ring."

There was no emotion in her voice and I couldn't tell how she meant this last comment, whether it included some kind of criticism or not. I tried to not to think about that and directed the conversation back to Gloria.

"She seems focused on me not having cancer anymore and that I shouldn't walk. She's incredibly intrusive."

"Not at all like you."

"What's that supposed to mean?"

"I think the first thing you asked me when you got here was why we were letting Robert take Ring with him. That wasn't intrusive?"

"It's different. That was about choice."

"Oh."

After a while, without looking up, Viviana said, "You could consider it. Since you can't really come to terms with Ring being sent away. Just a place to go temporarily, something to try. You went all the way to Churchill and didn't really see any of it. You didn't see a single goddamn polar bear. And you keep telling me you wish you'd created some kind of legacy for Rachel, that you wish you could figure out some way to do that before you walk. This could give you a chance to do that, maybe start the fund you were talking about. Why not go there and give yourself a time limit, maybe Ring's life, then come back if you want? Or come back sooner if you need to. I think about it, you know. Leaving with the idea of coming back if I need to."

We were silent again, and I started to feel restless.

"I can't imagine doing it. I really can't. But if I could imagine it, could you imagine doing it with me?"

Viviana visibly stiffened.

"Yeah," I said. "I didn't think so."

"The thought just made me anxious. That's all," she said. "But everything makes me anxious except the thought of staying here. That's the problem."

I considered this. "I'm not saying the hotel is a sane idea," I said. "I think it's completely nuts and I have no intention of doing it. But if you think about leaving, at least Churchill's not as far away as Atlanta. It's still in the snow, still away from everyone you knew, could still be about doing routines and with the option to come back here."

Viviana sighed. "I'm still leaning pretty heavily on Catherine and Samu. No offense, but you're not Catherine and Samu. You're not exactly stable, Lee. If we tried to live somewhere together, I'm afraid we'd both go downhill."

"Then we could come back."

"So now you think it's a good idea?"

"No," I said.

"You're depressed, Lee. You're depressed and I have anxiety. I'm afraid of being thrown back into panic attacks if I leave here. At least at this point… And I'm not sure that what we need is the same."

I leaned back against the side of the platform, an unfamiliar feeling washing over me. It wasn't despondence. It felt more like disappointment.

SERVICE

"Well, it's an interesting idea." Catherine was helping me fill the tub with ice the next afternoon. "Don't you think it's an interesting idea?"

"I don't know how interesting it is. I don't want to send Ring to the rescue. But I also can't see running a hotel or being able to live somewhere on my own for any length of time. Viviana seemed kind of interested but said she'd be too scared. Actually, I'm not even sure she seemed interested. She says I'm not stable. And I'm not…. And really, I have no interest either. I was just thinking about it. That's all."

"Lee, what makes you so afraid to try going there by yourself? Are you scared of being alone and depressed, anxious? Or are you afraid of letting yourself do something that's headed toward life? Because you've been doing things headed toward life the whole time you've been here. You may not think of it as heading toward life because you've been planning to walk, but you've been nourishing your body, healing it. Your body's been moving toward light, not darkness."

Catherine looked at me intensely, and I couldn't tell if it was out of concern or annoyance. When I arrived at the sanctuary, everything about her was gentle and calm, but now there was some other energy beneath her words. Samu was an open book, but I had trouble reading her.

She kept talking. "Your subconscious is being run by your routines here at this point. Whether or not you can admit it, that's living—you're living—despite yourself. Look at Ring. Ring lost his only person, he grieved, but he's not afraid to be alive. It doesn't mean he loved Robert any less."

"Ring wasn't Rachel's parent. Ring isn't human. And Ring couldn't have saved Robert."

Catherine raised her eyebrows. "Could you have saved Rachel?"

"I don't know. Maybe I could have. I didn't even try."

"So you can't save yourself?"

"It's not right to save myself."

"Is it right to help Ring?"

I reached up and touched my face and realized I was crying.

Catherine continued. "You get to choose what happens next. No matter what it feels like now, you didn't have control over Rachel dying. But you have control over what you do now. You can decide to try something. You can decide to do something no matter what. You can decide to think only about today or the next day. What you decide to focus on will create your state of being. It will condition your emotions. You have control over this. It may not feel like it, but you do."

She kept talking as I began to undress.

"Victor Frankl, who wrote *Man's Search for Meaning*, spent World War II in a Nazi concentration camp. In the space between what happens to you and how you react are your thoughts about what's happening. He experienced horrible abuse, but he realized no one could control what he thought. No one could make him think something he didn't want to. And this meant he could control his reactions. People sometimes survive unthinkable things. He survived a concentration camp. Many people didn't, but he did."

I looked down, through the blur of tears, and noticed that my legs didn't seem quite so alien anymore, that a small amount of muscle tone had returned.

"If you focus on why you can't survive, and keep repeating that over and over again," she went on, "you're training your brain to make that the way you see yourself, the way you see your life. If you focus instead on what you *will* do, what you *can* do, it will change your brain. It will change what you feel. But you need to be brave enough to allow that change, to not think that changing your feelings means letting go of Rachel. It doesn't mean letting go of her. It means taking her with you. If you're afraid to do that for yourself, and for Rachel, think about whether you can do it for someone else."

I was lowering myself into the ice water, exhaling strongly and slowly. The water stung.

"Maybe ask yourself if you can do it for Ring. Can you give Ring a life? No matter that there is suffering. No matter that he will die someday. No matter that you will die someday. No matter that Rachel did die. Can you just be here for him right now? What about tomorrow? Can you decide you'll do this for him and commit to that experience? If you can do that, it will change your mind. At this point, your mind is causing your suffering."

"Rachel's death is causing my suffering."

"Rachel's death is in the past. Rachel is not dying now. Your thoughts about Rachel's death are causing you to suffer."

"Rachel's death isn't in the past. Rachel's death is in the present."

"How is it in the present? Because she's absent? She was physically absent from you many times when she was alive too. But you didn't suffer then as you do now."

"That was different." My skin was getting bright red. I was losing count, wondering when to get out.

"Part of the difference is what you think, in your own mind, about not being able to see or talk to Rachel. The meaning you attach to that. Before, when you couldn't see or talk to her, you imagined her being somewhere living her life, and that you'd see her again in the future. You assumed she was there and would always be there. But you didn't actually know that; there was never any guarantee of that. You just thought it, and you believed your thoughts, and believing in the truth of your own thoughts kept you from suffering. What's different now is that you think she's dead."

"She *is* dead now." Maybe the temperature of the water was affecting my ability to understand what Catherine was saying, but she didn't seem to be making any sense.

"She's not dead here in front of you. What's different right now is that you think about her being dead. If you came here and she was alive, she would still be absent from you. She's with you as much now as she would be if she were still alive thousands of miles away in the desert and you were here. It's your thoughts that are different… that make you suffer."

A thousand miles. I needed to get out of the tub. I stood up.

"When she was away from you before, so far away from you, did you feel her presence? Did you know you could reach her if you wanted to?"

"I couldn't always reach her." I climbed out of the tub.

Catherine was right. She'd been a thousand miles from me frequently in the last years. What was different was that now I knew I'd never see her again.

And that she'd never grow old.

"She'll never grow old!" I shouted, startling myself. How could Catherine say there was no difference? That was a crazy way to view death. Maybe that's why they were able to spend their time helping people die. They had no concept of what it means to actually lose someone you really love."

"Horse stance," Catherine directed quietly but firmly.

I got into position and started the breathing exercises.

"Lee, she hadn't grown old then either. When she was alive and far away from you, you weren't even thinking about her growing old. Focusing on her not growing old now is a thought you're having. Our lives last as long as they last. The years she didn't have exist only in your mind. No one promised you she'd outlive you. No one could promise you that. She wasn't old then and she's not old now. You can't see her anymore, but you couldn't see her then either when she wasn't with you. You just knew she was somewhere else and you could bear that. You can bear it now if you decide to bear it. It's your mind that's making this current absence so different from earlier ones. It's your mind telling you it's forever.

"I'm not saying nothing happened to her. Something terrible happened to her. But it's not happening now, and she's still out there somewhere, and you can know she's out there the way you knew she was out there before. If you let yourself."

Catherine handed me my clothes and kept talking.

"The mother of one of the children killed in the Sandy Hook school shooting had to heal herself because she had another child to take care of. She did it in two ways. She looked for signs from her son who was killed. And she discovered the formula for healing. Gratitude plus forgiveness plus service to others. A Rwandan genocide survivor discovered this same formula. She visited her mother's killer in prison. She helped other survivors. Gratitude plus forgiveness plus service to others. People go through terrible things, Lee. Unimaginable things. There are a thousand ways to respond. But only one leads to healing."

"Maybe I don't want to heal." I was breathing hard again, even though I was out of the ice water.

"Maybe you don't want to heal. Maybe you do. You came here instead of taking your life at home. You came here. You did what I asked of you. Something has carried you along. And now you say that Gloria's made you this offer. Maybe you can find Rachel, find gratitude for Rachel. Maybe you can forgive—forgive whoever took Rachel's life, forgive the universe, forgive yourself. And maybe, just maybe, you have been given this gift by a dying woman who also lost a child—a way to be of service to others."

I looked at her skeptically. She gazed back at me with an expression that was again gentle, and said, "Maybe you can do that for Rachel, maybe you can survive and serve others as a legacy for her. I think that's part of what Gloria was trying to suggest. Or maybe you can use this opportunity as a place to live with Ring while you figure out another way to honor Rachel's memory. I know you're afraid. I know you're in pain. And I know maybe you don't want to heal. I just wonder if maybe you do."

I didn't have anything left to say. I finished dressing in silence and then took Ring back to our room to lie down. As I took off my boots, my eye caught the rocking chair with my backpack on it. Sticking out of a side pocket was the guidebook that Rachel and I had used so many months earlier to plan our trip. I felt like I wanted to open it and read it again, but I didn't know what I'd be looking for, or why I thought it would help.

RING

That night, while Viviana was clearing dinner, I went out to the platform with Ring. I didn't bring a blanket, just sat on the platform and pulled Ring to me. With one hand, I removed the glove from my other hand, pulled off my hood and hat, and ran my fingers through my hair. It was growing again, enough that it was coming down over my ears, and it felt like straw from the bar soap. I couldn't remember the last time I'd looked in a mirror.

I closed my eyes and imagined looking into one. Remembered how looking in the mirror is never exact, that what's on our right appears to be on our left. I covered my eyes and uncovered them. My eyes are green. I tried to remember the shade.

I put my glove back on and ran it through Ring's fur around his head. It felt dense through the glove. I touched his red coat. I remembered what his fur felt like, what his coat felt like, to my bare fingers. I looked at him.

"I'm terrified."

He licked my face.

"I see you." I turned my face away but he moved with it and continued to lick. "It's okay. I'm not letting you go. I'll take care of you, no matter what."

I held him to me and looked up at the sky. The tears were running again, and I tried to wipe them away with the glove of my other hand. I was freezing.

"Rachel, where are you?" I felt desperate, panicked. "Where are you?"

I held Ring to me and started rocking, slightly at first and then more pronounced. I rocked him, rocked myself. The moonlight shone on the snow around the platform so that it glowed a little. My ears were stinging. I pulled my hood up over my head and looked up at the sky.

And then the lights came.

ACKNOWLEDGMENTS

This book was written in isolation but expanded in community. I have so many people to thank that it's difficult to know where to start. But most writing is like that. You just need to begin.

Thank you to Bruce Bortz and Bancroft Press for believing in this book enough to put it out into the world. And for recognizing that the material it covers—death, grief, learning how to live without someone you love—are things that all of us have to face at some point but few of us know how to talk about. And that we need to have the conversations.

Thank you to my agent, Veronica Goldstein at UTA, for looking at a 48k word draft and seeing a novel in it. *Ring* would, quite literally, not be the story it is without your developmental edits and suggestions for deepening and broadening it.

Thank you to Steven Stinnett for encouraging me to write prose and to keep at it every day. You helped create the conditions through which this novel came into being.

Thank you to my mentor, Laura Boss, for being the only person I felt safe showing the very first draft to, and for answering my questions this way: "Yes, this counts as a novel, and yes, you should finish it."

Thank you to my amazing writing group—Debra Whittall, Megan Kidwell, and Bromme Cole— for reading the umpteenth draft and providing detailed and valuable feedback week after week (after week). And to Joan Dempsey for hosting the Gutsy Great Novelist community, from which our group developed, and for providing feedback on the early pages.

Thank you to Frank Busch, award-winning author of *Grey Eyes* (go get it and read it!) and its upcoming sequels, for providing helpful sensitivity reading, local flavor, and scene suggestions. Thank you also, Frank, for the sheer amount of time you spent giving me feedback and advice, not only about *Ring* but about the publishing world in general. You were the first person to tell me what an ARC is!

Thanks also to Sarah Wiebe, author of *Life Against States of Emergency*, for your careful review of the novel and your encouragement, and to Sarah Clark for your insights.

Because I'm neurotic and always need one more opinion, I have an awful lot of beta readers to thank. But every single one performed a huge service and helped move the book forward in important ways. Thank you to Lisa Monteleone and Stefanie Balandis for reading the whole thing twice. Thank you to Emmeline Chang, who not only helped me with sticky elements of the story but also gave me a primer every time I didn't understand a publishing term or requirement—all without making me feel like an idiot.

Thank you to Kimberly Bunker, Andrew Holz, Faith Dowgin, Jen Goellnitz, Donna Riley, Sharon Quiroz, Lillie Gardner, Chris Durost, Denise Poli, Sue Mortimer, and Gray Tuttle for reading drafts, being honest, and asking questions like "Why is Catherine such a know-it-all?" and "Does Matt ever talk about anything but politics?"

Thank you to Christine Van Bree for designing the cover with patience and artistry, and to Sean Tuttle-Lerner for helping me express my vision for it.

Thank you to Beth Staples of *Shenandoah* for publishing an excerpt from the novel and a craft essay on its writing (available at https://shenandoahliterary.org/thepeak/a-grief-explored/).

My gratitude goes as well to Peter Elliot and Matt Misetich at Pipeline Media Group for encouragement and assistance, and for recognizing the first draft of *Ring* as a finalist for the Pipeline Unpublished contest.

Many thanks also to the following publishers and contest administrators for awarding various versions of the manuscript with finalist status, longlisting, or other recognition: Dzanc Books, Bridge Eight Press, Fiction Five, ScreenCraft, and Gutsy Great Novelist. You gave me the confidence to pursue representation and publication and, in the process, change hats from poet to fiction writer.

I owe a huge debt of gratitude to the following authors, clinics, and health care providers who taught me about the context of suicidality, the embodiment of trauma, and the various modalities of healing—some by writing books, others by teaching classes, and some by actually treating me: Jennifer Michael Hecht, Dr. Bessel Van der Kolk, Dr. Gabor Maté, Dr. Bernie Siegel, Wim Hof, Amy Scher, The Optimum Health Clinic, and Sarah Borda.

Finally, thank you to my family for support, and to the animals in my life for getting me through each and every day, even the hard ones.

RESOURCES FOR FURTHER READING AND VIEWING:

GRIEF

"A Grief Explored" (on the writing of *Ring*): https://shenandoahliterary.org/thepeak/a-grief-explored

Modern Loss: https://modernloss.com/

Alliance of Hope (for suicide loss survivors): https://allianceofhope.org

SUICIDE

Stay: A History of Suicide and the Philosophies Against It (book) by Jennifer Michael Hecht

The Trevor Project: https://www.thetrevorproject.org/

NIMH hotline and resources: https://www.nimh.nih.gov/health/topics/suicide-prevention

EMBODIMENT OF TRAUMA

The Body Keeps the Score: Brain, Mind, and Body in the Healing of Trauma (book) by Bessel Van der Kolk

"All of Us Store Trauma in Our Bodies. Best-Selling Author and Trauma Expert Dr. Gabor Maté Shares How to Start Healing Today" by Gabor Maté in *Maria Shriver's Sunday Paper: https://www.mariashriversundaypaper.com/dr-gabor-mate/*

Healing Trauma: A Pioneering Program for Restoring the Wisdom of Your Body (book) by Peter Levine
"Peter Levine Demonstrates How Trauma Sticks in the Body" (video): https://www.youtube.com/watch?v=fiq0sILHiJs

HEALING MODALITIES FOR EMBODIED TRAUMA

How to Heal Yourself from Depression When No One Else Can (book) by Amy Scher

Yoga for Depression: A Compassionate Guide to Relieve Suffering Through Yoga (book) by Amy Weintraub

"Breathwork Is All the Rage Right Now, But Does It Work" by Juliane Bugmann: https://indigobluemagazine.com/breathwork-is-all-the-rage-right-now-but-does-it-work/

*The John Barnes Myofascial Release Approac*h (Website includes practitioner directory): https://myofascialrelease.com/

Wim Hoff Method: https://www.wimhofmethod.com/

"How to Tap with Jessica Ortner: Emotional Freedom Technique Informational Video": https://www.youtube.com/watch?v=pAclBdj20ZU

EFT International Directory of Practitioners: https://eftinternational.org/discover-eft-tapping/find-eft-practitioners/

USE OF THE WORD "SETTLER"

"

Settling on a Name: Names for non-Indigenous Canadians" by âpihtawikosisân/Chelsea Vowel:

https://apihtawikosisan.com/2020/02/settling-on-a-name-names-for-non-indigenous-canadians/

DECOLONIZATION

"Decolonization is not a metaphor" by Eve Tuck and K. Wayne Yang in *Decolonization: Indigeneity, Education & Society*:

https://jps.library.utoronto.ca/index.php/des/article/view/18630/15554

Safe Water for Attawapiskat and Other First Nations

"Safe Water Rights for First Nations" by The Council of Canadians:
https://canadians.org/fn-water/

"Troubled water: The slow drip of change in Attawapiskat is not and has never been enough" by Adrian Sutherland in *The Globe and Mail*:

https://www.theglobeandmail.com/opinion/
article-troubled-water-the-slow-drip-of-change-in-attawapiskat-is-not-and-has/

"Attawapiskat's Unsafe Water Emergency Has Been My Normal For 42 Years" by Adrian Sutherland in *HuffPost Canada*:

https://www.huffpost.com/archive/ca/entry/
attawapiskat-unsafe-water-emergency_ca_5d445656e4b0ca604e313c01

Shannen Koostachin and Educational Rights for First Nations Children

Shannen's Dream: https://fncaringsociety.com/shannens-dream

Hi-Ho Mistahey! (movie) directed by Alanis Obomsawin: https://www.youtube.com/watch?v=3uWHrw4glqU

Perspectives from Attawapiskat/ Critique of media coverage of Attawapiskat

Reimagining Attawapiskat project (photos and video):
https://www.reimaginingattawapiskat.com/

The People of the Kattawapiskak River (movie) directed by Alanis Obomsawin
https://www.nfb.ca/film/people_of_kattawapiskak_river/

Treaty Relations, States of Emergency, and the Idle No More Movement

Inspired by Attawapiskat Chief Theresa Spence

The Winter We Danced: Voices from the Past, the Future, and the Idol No More Movement (book) by the Kino-nda-niimi Collective

Life against States of Emergency: Revitalizing Treaty Relations from Attawapiskat (book) by Sarah Marie Wiebe

CALL TO ACTION

Half of the author royalties from this book will be donated to Shannen's
Dream to support the educational rights of
First Nations children.

Please further support Shannen's Dream by donating at:
https://fncaringsociety.com/donate
(use the drop-down menu to specify Shannen's Dream campaign)

Please support The Trevor Project's suicide prevention work at:
https://give.thetrevorproject.org/give/63307/#!/donation/checkout

ABOUT THE AUTHOR

Michelle Lerner is a multi-faceted talent whose journey has traversed the fields of law, poetry, and now fiction. She began her academic career at Princeton University, where she graduated summa cum laude in 1993 with an AB in Anthropology. She continued her education at Harvard Law School, earning her JD magna cum laude in 1998. Not one to rest on her laurels, Michelle also acquired an MFA in Poetry from The New School in 2008.

She worked diligently for over twenty years as a public interest lawyer. Her life took an unforeseen detour when she was diagnosed with the neurological form of Lyme Disease, putting her on a multi-year path to recovery. This challenging period became a crucible for her creative transformation. Unable to continue her law career, she delved into fiction, writing her debut novel "Ring." The book, slated for publication next year, incorporates her personal experience with chronic illness, although it ventures into realms of imagination she never explored in her legal briefs or her poetry.

Michelle has received numerous accolades for her work across different mediums. Notable among these are her quarterfinalist position in the ScreenCraft Cinematic Book Competition 2023, being a finalist for multiple fiction prizes including the 2020 Book Pipeline Unpublished Contest, and being longlisted for various awards such as the Dzanc Prize for Fiction. Her poetry manuscripts have also earned her a semi-finalist spot for the Pamet River Prize and Willow Run Poetry Book Award.

In the world of poetry, Michelle's work has been published in numerous journals like the Virginia Quarterly Review, Connecticut River Review, and LIPS. Her poetry chapbook "Protection" was published by Poetry Box and one of its poems received a Pushcart Prize nomination. She's also had the honor of being nominated for the Pushcart Prize and Best New Poets for other poems.

Michelle's commitment to community is evident in her service roles. She currently serves as the Executive Director and Board Member of the Laura Boss Poetry Foundation. She also mentors for the organization "We Are Not Numbers," providing guidance to young writers.

As a seasoned public speaker, Michelle has featured in diverse forums including the Delaware Valley Poetry Festival, as well as regional, national, and international conferences.

She resides in New Jersey with her family, where she also runs a cat rescue. Her upcoming projects include a collection of humorous personal essays about the opinionated animals she has lived with. In her downtime, Michelle strums a guitar and composes songs that she sings anywhere no one will hear her.

To explore more of Michelle's diverse body of work, you can visit her website at michellelerner.net.